Stories (Within)

An Anthology of Stories Within Stories

Within Stories Within Stories Within Stories
Within Stories Within Stories Within Stories
Within Stories Within Stories Within Stories
Within Stories Within Stories Within Stories
Within Stories Within Stories Within Stories
Within Stories Within Stories Within Stories
Within Stories Within Stories Within Stories

by Benjamin Gorman
Mark Teppo
Rick M. Cook
Karen Eisenbrey
Barb Lachenbruch
Susan Hammerman
Frances Lu-Pai Ippolito
LM Zaerr
Dr. Bunny McFadden
Ann Ornie
Debby Dodds
Gabby Gilliam
Benjamin Gorman
Gabby Gilliam
Debby Dodds
Ann Ornie
Dr. Bunny McFadden
LM Zaerr
Frances Lu-Pai Ippolito
Susan Hammerman
Barb Lachenbruch
Karen Eisenbrey
Rick M. Cook
Mark Teppo
and Benjamin Gorman

Published in the United States by
Not a Pipe Publishing, Independence, Oregon.
www.NotAPipePublishing.com

Paperback Edition

ISBN-13: 978-1-956892-13-0

Contents

Storytellers

by Benjamin Gorman

My best story? Okay, take a seat.

I'm Zora. What's your name?

Nice to meet you. Well, Danique, you're going to want to get comfortable for this one. It's a long one. Worth it? Well, that will be up to you, I guess. But it's my favorite. Maybe the most important one I've heard, so when people ask for the best, it's my go-to. But it's a tricky one. I'll be up front about that. Gotta listen carefully. Here, pull up a stool and get me a drink.

Hmm. What do you have that's good for sipping slowly? We're gonna be here for a bit.

Yeah, that sounds good. I'll have one of those over ice.

Okay, you're going to have to drink enough for both of us to rent these barstools. No, don't be scared; it's not *that* long. And it's worth it. I promise.

So, the first thing you need to know about my home planet, Luyten b, is that it has four little moons. When I'm working these long hauls and run into people from planets with no moons, or only one moon, they don't understand how moons work. I mean, intellectually they get them, but they don't understand that they don't all rise and set at the same time each day. Sometimes there's only one in the sky. Sometimes there are all four. Mostly just two or three, because the others are on the other side, right. So it becomes kind of an event when you have a night where three or four rise at the same time. And my grandfather, he's retired. He has the time to pay attention to that kind of thing. So when there's a night that three or four moons will be rising, he sends me a message and asks me to come over and watch with him. He's done this since I was a little girl, way before I got into shipping and started leaving for long hauls. And with the time dilation, he's getting a lot older a lot faster than he was when I was a kid. So every time I go back, I make a point to try to get over there to see him. I've been gone for a month or two, but he's missed me for years. And he's been getting ready to see me. He gets ready by collecting stories. Yeah, it's sweet. I love him.

People say Grandpa Vic is the best storyteller. He has a reputation for it, and not just in our town. I'll meet people lightyears away, and they'll say, "Wait, you're Vic's granddaughter? That guy is the best storyteller." And he's never even been off-world, but they invariably ran into him at some bar like this one when he was young, and he told them a story, and they remember him decades later. And always fiction. Never true stories like this one. He doesn't collect other people's most interesting personal experiences like a zookeeper of human lives. "There's still too much slavery in the universe, self-imposed and otherwise, and I don't want to contribute to that," he says. So he doesn't take people's lives. He takes what they make and give away. Made up stories. Some new. Some very old. But all fiction. And it's not just about freedom. "You find the truth through fiction, but not the other way around," he says. It's like a religion for him, almost, but one built on *dis*belief. That's Grandpa Vic.

Some people will say he's a natural storyteller, like it's something in the blood, or a roll of the dice at birth. And maybe. I think maybe he'd agree with that. But not the way they mean. He gets lots of practice, and he works at it. Studies it, you know? And I mean "it," not "them." Sure, he learns these stories, but he studies "story." The *idea* of story. That's what makes him good at telling them. He knows how a story is supposed to work. And he has this theory about why they work. It's no big secret, but it's hard to fully understand. But one night, he explained it to me, and I think I got it.

I'd come back from this long run, almost three months my time, must have been seven or eight years for him. Once we got the hauler unloaded, I received my shore leave, so I went back to visit my parents first, and my mom told me her dad had been leaving these urgent messages. She thought it was kind of funny he was so eager to make sure I came over right away. She gets it, but she thinks it's cute, too. She's not into the moonrises like he is. But she knows I am. She knows he got me hooked when I was little.

Of course, I took off over there that very evening so I wouldn't miss it. All four moons coming up over the horizon almost at the same time. Very rare. He was so excited, when I got to his house, we didn't even sit down. He gave me a real quick hug and then said, "C'mon! C'mon!" and hustled me right through to the back door, then out to our spot. Luyten b is rocky, and there's still not much that grows outdoors. He's got this plot of land that's big and mostly empty. About a hundred meters from his back door, there's this sheer drop-off into a deep valley. He's set up a fire pit on the edge, and a little half-ring of folding chairs that he never folds and takes back inside. When we got out there, he already had the firepit going. It's a fake one, of course. Like I said, not much grows on Luyten b. It would be stupid to burn wood. But his fire pit looks pretty real when you turn it on, and it produces more heat than a real fire, if you want it to. He also had a pair of thermoses of coffee ready and waiting. His coffee is bad. As famously bad as his storytelling is good, almost. But I've never told him so. He used to let me drink coffee when I was way too young, just so I could stay up and watch the moons with him, and that felt special, so it's part of the ritual now.

We got out there and took our seats just as the sun was setting. Luyten's Star is a little red dwarf, and the atmosphere on Luyten b doesn't have much moisture, even after the terraforming, so the sunsets aren't pretty like on lots of other worlds. Just very clear. But that clarity means, when the moons come up, they're all so bright and crisp. Like you could reach out and run a finger across them and feel the texture of each one. The first was already over the horizon way off to the south of us, like it got a head start before the gun went off, but the next three came up after sunset, not quite at the same time, but just one, two, three. None would eclipse another that night. They all rotate at their own speeds, so they would cross each other's paths, but the horizon line was the closest they'd get to each other. Moon gazing is slow business, but that first half an hour, we just watched in near silence, enjoying the show.

"I've got a story for you, Zora," Grandpa said.

I knew he'd been sitting on it. I could have asked, but it was nice to make him squirm a little. He was 240 years old at that point. It's good to let somebody that old be giddy with excitement. Keeps 'em young.

"Is it a good one?"

"It's an important one," he said.

Now that was unusual. Grandpa tells stories to entertain. He puts on a show. But he doesn't preach. Not most of the time. He's self-indulgent, sure. But like an actor who wants to give a monologue, not a teacher who wants to make you remember a lesson.

"Why so?"

He looked down into the valley in front of us. The moons had lit up the tops of the mountains on the other side just enough to make out the faint blue glows of each point, stacked one in front of the other, ridges of brown rock by day that had become an unmoving ocean of moonlight. "Do you ever wonder how we got here, Zora? How we made it this far out? Not you and me. All of us. And all the people you meet on your runs. There were a million chances to stop. To give up. To stay put or die or kill each other and be killed and never make it here. A billion chances. Maybe a nearly infinite number of tiny decisions made by billions of people just like you and me. Or completely different from you and me. But they made the choices that got us here. So how did we keep going? What was the secret?"

Now, if I'd wanted to be really mean, I could have told him a dozen different answers I'd come across in my life. For conquest. For profit. For land. To escape Earth. To escape other people. God's will. This god or that god or it's all god and it's destiny. There are lots of theories about what motivates human beings, and I'm cynical enough to suspect the theory you pick says more about you than the universe. I also have met enough missionaries selling me on their theory to know that when somebody asks you if you have accepted their particular lord and savior into your heart, they aren't asking for your story. They're asking if they can tell you theirs.

"What do you think, Grandpa?"

"Have you ever seen a nesting doll?" he asked.

That wasn't what I was expecting, either. I'd seen nests before. I'd been to planets where they had birds who lived in the wild and built nests, but I don't like to rub people's noses in that fact when I'm back home unless they ask. Some people can't afford to travel, and some choose not to, but even the ones who could and choose not to feel a little resentment when they're reminded about all the things they haven't seen because they've stayed put. And, of course, I'd had dolls when I was little. Come to think of it, I've never been to a planet where kids don't play with dolls. That's part of it all, I guess. The beginnings of learning about story. Telling them to ourselves. But I'd never heard of nesting dolls. Have you ever seen one? No, that's what I pictured, too. A doll in a nest. Or a robot doll that builds a nest, maybe. But that's not what they are.

"They go all the way back to Earth," Grandpa explained. "They were made of wood at first, then plastic, then thin plazcrete, but they always looked about the same. They don't look like normal dolls, more like barrels with rounded tops, and the image of a person is painted on the outside. Sometimes the same person on every one, and sometimes different people. They're impractical as dolls go. Not soft and not good representations of the human form. But what makes them interesting to children … and to grandparents mostly, and good metaphors for adults, and good subjects for political cartoonists …" He chuckled at this joke that made no sense to me. "What makes them interesting is that they are each a slightly different size than the last, and they open up in the middle, so you can fit one inside the next, inside the next, until all of them fit into the biggest one. They're more decorations than real toys, I guess, but ..."

His voice trailed off. We watched the moons in silence. I knew he was going somewhere with this, but I couldn't tell where. Like the moons. When you look at them for an instant, you know they have a path, but you can't tell what it is unless you wait to see it.

"Do you know what an ouroboros is, Zora?"

I didn't have the slightest guess for that one. I just shook my head.

"It's a symbol. Very, very old. Not old like your Grandpa is old. Ancient. Older than nesting dolls, probably. Back on Earth, they had them carved into their temples and tombs thousands of years before the last people left the planet for good. It looks like a snake, but it's in the shape of a circle with only this little bump and break where the head is biting the snake's own tail. We don't know exactly what it meant to them. Most of the scholars I've read say it meant eternity. But some have other ideas. Some say it's a kind of barrier, with chaos on the outside and order on the inside, and the snake is eating itself as a symbol of the renewal that's necessary to keep disorder out and make an orderly world inside. And maybe they're right. Maybe it's about a periodic renewal. Or maybe it's continuous. Maybe it is destroying itself and creating itself all the time because that's what we have to do to make sense of the world, to shape the space inside into something we can understand."

Silence again.

Finally, I bit.

"Okay, so is your story about a nesting doll or a snake biting its own tail? Or both? I'm confused, but you've piqued my interest." I laughed. "Tell me the damned story, Grandpa!"

He smiled and nodded, but I was quieted by his seriousness. "It doesn't start with a snake or a doll. It starts like this ..."

The Tale of the Tape

by Mark Teppo

She comes in through the tiny window under the peaked gable. The room is a narrow bedroom, and judging by the worn quilt on the bed and the shabby frown of the curtains, it wasn't occupied. After easing the window shut behind her, she crouches next to the wall for a minute, listening. Beside her, the radiator gurgles. Wood creaks overhead—the roof sighing in the cold damp of the night. Downstairs, a grandfather clock marches resolutely along—*tock, tock, tock*. Like a sandpiper stalking the beach.

Regular nighttime noises. The house is undisturbed. No one has noticed her entry.

The house is second from the left in a row of five. Brick and plaster. The sort of construction that would settle in the mud before falling over—a topic of increasing concern among homeowners the past dozen years or so. The seas kept creeping closer, the waves slowly grinding against the dikes and bulwarks generations had raised against the water.

She didn't share the locals' concern about the sea. Her concern was more immediate. These houses were stacked tightly together; you could barely fit a brick between each. If you were intent on entering one of these houses, there was no 'side window that looked out over a neglected garden' option. You had to enter through the front or the back, and both were exposed.

After watching the house for a few days, she had decided the high window was the best choice. She had never seen a light in the window, and branches from a tall oak planted next to the pedestrian bridge of the canal obscured the peak of the roof. As long as she moved carefully and quietly, she wouldn't attract any attention.

She was good at being quiet.

"Why that house?" Remejin had wanted to know when she had pointed it out to him a week earlier.

She showed him the book she had stolen from the library, tapping the name on the cover.

"The storyteller?" Remejin wrinkled his nose. "Man like that won't have any stones or strands. He's a popular one, that fellow, but he's not wealthy."

She shook her head. *Not gold*, she signed. She put two fingers against her throat.

Remejin gave her a look. "What? Like, in a bottle or something?"

She shrugged.

"You'll be disappointed," Remejin said. "What you want isn't possible. All he'll have is costume jewelry. Maybe some gold." He shook his head. "He's popular," he repeated. "Folks like him. Word gets out that you thieved him and ..."

I won't say anything, she signed.

Remejin laughed. "No, girl, I don't suppose you will."

There is a set of wooden stairs outside the attic bedroom. She takes her time, lightly placing one foot and then easing her weight forward. The wood absorbs her weight easily—she is a compact woman, after all, especially after cutting off all of that hair. It was a beautiful color, fiery like the sun when it burned against the edge of the sky, and once upon a time, it flowed about her like a silky cloud. She had barely noticed it. But that hadn't been the case since she came to this island.

The third step from the bottom is older than the others, and it groans slightly when she steps on it. She pauses, holding her breath. Listening.

Downstairs, the grandfather clock is steady. *Tock. Tock. Tock.* Time moving on, uncaring.

Remejin had found her abandoned on the shore, naked and shivering. Her eyes pale like an old shell; her lips, cold and blue. He had wrapped her (and her hair) in his cloak and brought her back to his windowless room behind the basement boilers. He packed her snugly in a wooden crate with blankets stolen from the nursery down the road. She refused to eat, but he was patient, and eventually, she would accept weak broth from a chemist's dropper. Soon, she could hold a teacup on her own, and he would sit on the floor and watch her.

Soon after, he started telling her stories, getting her used to the sound of his voice. Hoping that his words would spark something in her brain that would allow her to talk.

She never did, but she learned to communicate with her hands.

You have very nimble fingers, he had said one day, and, being a thief of some renown, he had a use for her and her fingers.

She grew stronger. Her eyes darkened. Her lips were no longer cold and blue. Her hair regained its luster. And her fingers, well, her fingers were even more nimble than the old thief anticipated.

The grandfather clock is carved in the likeness of an old man. He towers over her, a cloaked figure with a face like a cracked cliff. His beard is long, and it curls down one edge of the glass case that fills his belly. He has one hand raised, his fingers frozen forever in a gesture like he was about to pluck an apple from a tree. Someone—the storyteller, most likely—has draped a heavy ribbon around his wrist. Suspended from the ribbon is a heavy medal.

She peers at the ornament. *For services to the mythopoetic arts*, it says. The heavy letters circle a quill laid over a piece of parchment. She touches the medal, and it spins slowly. On the back is the grim-faced visage of the old king—the seal of the Kingdom. He has a passing resemblance to Old Grandfather, but then all elderly sages look the same, don't they? There is a paucity of vision among artists, a laziness that keeps them returning to what is well known.

Of course, this might explain why the storyteller is so beloved. His stories were different, unlike anything that had been told before.

"Once upon a time ..." That was how he started his stories, and with those four words, he could stop time. He could silence a room full of noisy children. He could make grown women forget their husbands. He could make heads of state hold their tongues. "Once upon a time ..." was all it took.

Remejin was under no illusions about his skills as a storyteller. His voice was too harsh, ravaged by years of smoke and sea spray. He had fallen too many times, and his back was stiffer than an aged oak that had been blasted by lightning. He didn't like making faces. But he could make his fingers dance. What he lacked in physical grace and animation in his features, he made up for with his hands. Position a light just right, and he could make shadows move on the wall. He could create men on horseback, galloping off to fight in battle; wolves, howling at a sallow moon; and princesses slipping out of high windows, intent on grand adventures. Once, she had seen him contort his fingers in such a way as to create a shadow dragon with scaly wings.

She didn't use her fingers to make shadow puppets. She used her fingers to suggest words. To express derision with the crook of a little finger. To laugh with a palm and outstretched fingers. To communicate the number of guards and their route through the dimly lit halls of a national museum. Remejin was the only one who could understand her stories, and for a few years, it was enough.

Until the day when she first saw the storyteller. When she first heard him tell his most famous story.

"Once upon a time, there was a girl who lived in the sea ..."

And that was when she decided to steal his most precious treasure.

She slips into the library like a breath of night wind. The only illumination is a thin slice of moonlight, a bright slash across the heavy rug. It is enough light, however, for her to discern shapes and forms. The room is lined with bookcases. There is a desk near the heavily-curtained windows, and some kind of machine sits on the desk. The walls are filled with bookcases, except for a large oil painting that hangs on the wall opposite the windows. She stays close to the bookcases, her fingers trailing lightly across the rugged leather of the spines. Remejin would have been distracted by all the books. *Imagine the stories.* She can almost hear him whispering in her ear. He would linger overlong, plucking out a volume here and there. Holding them near the moonlight so as to read their contents. He would be unable to decide which to take, and such indecision, she knew, would be his undoing. When the sun chased the moon away, Remejin would still be here, in the library of old books, trying to decide which story to steal.

She only wants one, and she knows it won't be found in any of the books on the shelves. It is not the sort of story that could be transcribed onto coarse vellum and wrapped in the tanned hide of a dead animal.

She finds the safe behind the painting. The picture frame—carved in a tangled confusion of branches and covered in gold—is mounted on a hinge, and it comes away from the wall with the slightest tug. Set in the wall, hidden from the moon's sight, is the hard and heavy safe.

It has a combination dial, and had she had more patience, she might have watched the storyteller long enough to learn the sequence of numbers that would open the safe. But such surveillance takes time and luck, and she relied on neither.

Making the rest of her body still, she strokes the dial of the safe; her fingers—nimble and sensitive— would be enough.

There was a story Remejin could be cajoled into telling, should you catch him in his cups. *Tell us the story of the general's watch*, knowing patrons of the Magpie's Charm would beg. Remejin would feign ignorance, of course, because it is dangerous to brag of one's exploits, but the hidden room at the Charm was a safe place. You had to know how to find the hidden latch in the storeroom to gain entry, and they had all sworn an oath of secrecy. No, the back room was a sanctuary for thieves and burglars to tell the true stories of their profession. In that room, they could confess their sins and be rewarded with drink and cheer about their exploits.

Tell us the story of the general's watch, the crowd would beg of Remejin, and the master thief would finally relent. *Okay, okay, you blackhearted bastards*, he would say. *Gather 'round and listen.* And a hush would fall over the room, and ears and eyes would turn toward the stiff old oak with the fingers that could make the shadows dance.

This one, she could steal the breath from a butterfly, he would start. On the wall behind him, a shadowy figure would flutter. *Her touch was lighter than the kiss of a fairy ...*

She turns the dial on the safe a little more, and deep within the heavy box, a flywheel clicks. A metal tooth descends, freeing another wheel, and a weighted bar drops. It makes a noise like a brick landing on a paving stone, and she leans away from the safe, listening.

In the hall, the grandfather clock doesn't miss a step. *Tock. Tock. Tock.* The roof settles with a slight groan.

In the bedroom at the other end of the hall from the library, the man in the bed does not move. He remains deep in his slumber.

She grips the handle of the safe. She tugs it down, and it moves. The safe gasps, surprised to have given up its secrets so easily to the thief. She pulls the door open. The inside of the safe is dark—the moon, try as it might, cannot peer around the frame of the oil painting—but she doesn't need any light. Her touch—lighter than the kiss of a fairy—is enough.

There is only one object in the safe. A narrow box, square and thin. She lifts it out, and crouching near the lower edge of the painting, she opens it.

Inside is a reel of magnetic tape.

The machine on the desk is a device that will play the tape. She has never used such a machine, but she intuits how it works quickly enough. She threads the tape around the pegs and lays it across the vocalizing tongue. She binds the end onto the other reel, and like she is stroking the fur on the back of a badger, she adjusts the tension in the tape.

Before she starts the machine, she pauses for a second. *Are you sure?* She imagines Remejin's voice.

She presses the button. She has never been more sure of anything in her life.

The machine clacks into place, the tongue pressing up against the staple. The reels start turning. A voice issues from a tiny speaker in the machine. Listen, this is the story the voice tells …

Kanareyka

by Rick M. Cook

I'm making this recording to capture the truth before the memory softens, as if it ever could. It happened when I was fourteen, and it forever changed my life. As a young girl, I didn't have many life experiences, so please, hear me out before judging me.

It was just about a dozen years ago. Me and my mom were living in West Virginia, bumfuck nowhere. The neighbor boys Jimmy and Freddy tapped on my apartment's bedroom window one August night, right after my mom left me alone for her twelve-hour shift at the all-night diner. They wanted to explore some caves they'd heard about at school, which sounded way more fun than trying to sleep while it was hotter than Hell. Plus, it was the chance I'd been waiting for, to be in the dark with Jimmy Wilson, the undisputed king of my *Hot or Not* list. If geeky Freddy had to come along, too, well, it wasn't great. More of a nuisance, really. But sometimes, you gotta take what you're given.

After grabbing a bottle of water, I locked the apartment door behind me.

Freddy Davis, the nerdy, ever-prepared boy scout, brought a flashlight, a cartographer's map, some granola bars, a trowel, and a heavy coat. Jimmy, a spitting image of Ian Somerhalder, complete with smoldering eyes and bad-boy attitude, brought weed and three cans of beer.

In his short-sleeved shirt, Jimmy pointed at Freddy's supplies and scoffed. "You gonna dig us a tunnel to Antarctica?"

Freddy shuffled his feet. "Could be cold in there. And this," he said, holding up the small hand tool, "is in case we find any gold or silver veins." He smiled and looked to me for confirmation of his reasoning, but I only shrugged.

Jimmy laughed. "You're such a nimrod, Davis. It's a coal mine, and it's been cleaned out. But it might be a cool place to hang out and smoke some joints."

Jimmy was a year older than Freddy and me, but he'd been held back a grade. The summer had been kind to Jimmy. He was taller, his tanned arms were all muscle, and his jeans fit just right. I struggled to *not* stare at his dimples, light blue eyes, and perfect teeth. Some people were born lucky, never having to wear braces. Jimmy was that guy. And he knew it. At school, we orbited in different circles. I think we were only friends because of proximity, too far from the cool kids who lived deeper in the richer neighborhoods.

Freddy, on the other hand, was a lanky, pimple-faced kid who was always trying to fit in. The Davis family adopted him from Russia when he was seven, half his life ago, and they gave him just about anything he asked for, which wasn't much. If I'd been in his shoes, I would've milked that cow. But I think he feared being sent back to Russia or something …

We walked for about an hour, guided by a full moon and my iPhone's Google maps.

"This should be it," Freddy said finally, passing his flashlight over a huge outcropping of loose stones at the base of a large hill. It looked as if a giant had dropped a ton of rock at a random spot next to the mountain. The only clue that something had once been there was the gravel road that dead-ended into it, and most of that was overgrown with weeds.

Jimmy climbed over the larger rocks. "Are you sure, Freddy? I don't see any—oh, wait. Here!" He pointed, sunk to his knees, and disappeared.

Freddy and I scrambled to follow him. I flicked on my iPhone's flashlight.

"Jimmy, where are you?" I called.

A hand shot out from a small opening and grabbed my jeans. I screamed.

Jimmy's face peered from the opening. "You gotta crawl in on your knees. A rockslide covered most of the opening. But this is it. C'mon in, Mandy." He reached up and tugged on my belt loop.

It was a good thing Jimmy couldn't see my face with my light in his eyes. It had flushed hot. It was the first time Jimmy had ever touched me on purpose, and I thought I'd die from the pounding in my chest.

Inside the cave, the rock walls were rough-cut, showing many tool marks. Dampness from the rain earlier in the evening set a chill in the air. With his coat on, Freddy was definitely the smartest of us, but I already knew that.

About hundred yards into the darkness, the tunnel split in two. The right branch dead-ended after a short decline into a coal-loading area. Above that area, a dome provided ample room from an upper level to dump coal into a chute that stopped on our level. Fist-sized chunks of coal cluttered the ground. Two rusty shovels leaned against the wall.

We backtracked and took the left branch and discovered a set of rails with an old mining cart still on the track. Boxes marked "Tamptite – High

Explosives" littered an alcove. Jimmy was the first one there, digging through them.

"Shit. Ain't nothing here but cobwebs and rat poop," he said, the flashlight catching his grimace.

If Jimmy thought he'd find anything in those ancient boxes, he was nuts. I looked over at Freddy. He must have been thinking the same thing because he rolled his eyes. When he caught me watching him, he sheepishly smiled.

We moved deeper into the tunnel.

It split again, and then again. Freddy had suggested, based on his Dungeons and Dragons experience into "uncharted realms," that we always keep taking the left fork. When it dead ended, we'd retrace our steps and, coming out of the tunnel, the next unexplored part of the complex would, again, be on our left. That way, we'd be able to explore all the tunnels and not get lost.

If only it had been that simple.

We passed another alcove with a small pile of electrical conduit, but the tunnel abruptly ended, its rails dangling over a deep dark cave. At the ledge, Freddy's powerful flashlight showed roughly hewn steps descending into the darkness. Jimmy jumped down to them without a care. The exploring had been fun, but my Spidey-Sense was tingling. Standing on the precipice, something told me not to go down there, to stay put, to go home. I wanted no part of that cave.

"C'mon, guys," Jimmy whined from twenty feet below us. "Don't wuss out on me."

How could he see without Freddy shining the light down there? It creeped me out. If he fell and broke something, how would we get him out of there?

"Jimmy, I'm cold," I said. "Can we go explore something else?"

Freddy was quick to agree, mostly because he had a crush on me and probably thought agreeing with me would win him points. It did. I knew about his crush earlier in the year when a mutual friend dished me the deets on him. He was nice but too geeky for me and not popular. On the other hand, Jimmy had been my crush since seventh grade. He was gorgeous and confident but could be a real pain in the ass. This was one such time, and it pissed me off.

Jimmy ignored me and climbed down another five feet. "I'll bet nobody's explored this huge cave. C'mon …"

"You guys do what you want," I said. "I'm going back." I turned and headed back to the pile of electrical pipe, guided by my iPhone's light.

Freddy pulled his light from the cave to highlight my way. Jimmy cursed in the darkness below. "Freddy, you shithead! I can't see."

Unsure what to do, Freddy froze for a few seconds. Jimmy called again from the darkness. "Freddy, dude, maybe there's a dragon down here. Wouldn't it be cool if you were the first to discover it?"

Freddy was always trying to fit in, but even he had his pride. Making fun of his love for D&D was taking

Kanareyka by Rick M. Cook

it too far. "You dumbass prick," Freddy mumbled. Then more loudly, he added, "You heard the lady. She's cold. Come on back up."

Freddy twisted in place to shine the light once more in my direction. I mouthed a "Thank you" to him and stepped around a large boulder.

We both heard Jimmy cursing in the darkness and the unmistakable sound of a Zippo lighter cap being flicked open.

"No!" Freddy shouted and ran at me. "Methane may—"

The explosion deafened me.

When I woke, absolute darkness and silence surrounded me. I scrambled to find my iPhone and flicked on its light. *Holy fuck.*

The tunnel was completely unrecognizable. Parts of it had collapsed all around me, shutting off my escape. Loose rock and pieces of coal littered the floor. Right behind me, the large boulder had luckily shielded me from the blast, but my ears rang. The smell of burnt hair and skin made me cringe. Struggling to breathe, I cupped a hand to my mouth and nose and panned the light through the millions of dust motes hanging in the air, back to where Jimmy and Freddy were, or rather, where they'd been.

"Jimmy?" I called. "Freddy?"

A wall of solid rock blocked the entire cave opening as if it had calved from a glacier higher up, slamming into the ledge Jimmy had been standing on. There could be no surviving that. He'd either fallen to his death or the giant stone had crushed him in an instant.

"Jimmy!" I yelled, my voice cracking. "Freddy! Where are you guys?"

An unearthly scream came from a new pile of rock covering the rails. The stump of an arm stuck out from it and shook frantically in the air, throwing blood in arcs. Just below that, I could make out Freddy's blistered and lacerated face.

"Oh my God, Freddy! Oh my God!"

I hobbled to his side and began moving rocks and stones as fast as I could from around his head. But his arm—*Jesus, his left arm*— had been sheared off just below the elbow, clumps of downy feathers from his coat stuck to the stub that remained like some sick crimson plumage. A nasty slash across his burned forehead streamed blood into his hair and eyes.

"Hold on, Freddy," I said, fighting the urge to throw up. "Hold on!" If he replied, I couldn't hear it.

I slipped the belt from my jeans, then strapped it tight to his left biceps just above the stump. There wasn't a hole punched that far down the belt, so I doubled the strap back on itself and tied it tight, as best I could.

Freddy shouted something incoherent at me, twisting his head in agony. My heart thumped in my ears, blocking out his words, while my mind raced trying to think of something I could do. I remember his eyes, bulging and wild with panic, full of fear.

"Pull me out," he yelled, his face scrunched up in terrible pain. "Ow, ow—" His voice broke into a long guttural howl, like that of an animal caught in a bear trap.

I grabbed his right hand and pulled, but slipped in the bloody mess around him. His body refused to move from the pile of rocks.

"Stop, stop!" He cried out again and moaned.

I let go immediately and knelt beside him. Some sort of thick pipe poked my leg, so I grabbed it to move it. My hand came up holding Freddy's severed left forearm with his hand still attached. I shrieked, tossed it away, but couldn't hold back any longer. I puked my guts up.

"It hurts … it hurts," Freddy said between gasps. He spat a bunch of words at me in Russian, words that sounded like curses, and swiped at his forehead, smearing the wound there into a gory mess.

I wiped my mouth, tore off my long sleeves, and fashioned a bandage for his forehead. The water I'd brought worked okay to clean his wounds and rinse my mouth of vomit.

"That burns," he cried, with eyelids squeezed shut. Fresh tears pooled in the corners of his eyes.

I pressed the cloth to his forehead, trying to get the gash to clot. "I'm sorry, Freddy. What else can I do?"

"Get me out!" he screamed and lost consciousness, the pain too great for him.

After a few minutes, he woke and began to whimper and moan again. His breathing became less panicked. He placed the crook of his right elbow over his face and half-coughed, half-sobbed. His chest heaved with the exertion while sweat beaded on his forehead. Paralyzed, I knelt there, my mind empty of rational thought but full of dread.

Was I going to die here? Would he be able to walk out of the tunnel? What if he couldn't? Was he going to die? I couldn't let that happen to him, but I felt so useless.

"Hang on, Freddy," I said, brushing his cheek. "You're not going to die on me, are you?"

Shit, what the fuck was I saying? Talk less, do more.

"Of course, you're not," I added and pulled the trowel from his supply bag. "Don't worry, I've got a plan."

The shovels we saw earlier would've been a huge help, but they were on the other side of the cave-in, unreachable. Using my hands and the tiny trowel, I cleared all the pebbles and small stones from around his shoulders, chest, and waist. When tugging at the larger rocks below that, I soon found I couldn't move the biggest one crushing his pelvis and legs. It was as large as the one that sheltered me from the explosion.

Everything below his waist was flattened. There was Freddy, his stomach, his belt, and then just … rock. Like he'd been squirted out from under a giant slab.

How could he even be alive as a half-person? Jesus Christ, don't say that. Don't even think it.

I bowed my head, dug my fingers under the rock, and let a small cry out as I heaved. The stone didn't budge. "Fuck! I can't … I can't lift it."

He's never going to walk again.

"I'm so sorry, Freddy." I wanted to give up, but then another idea hit me. "Just hang on."

I dug into the earth where the crushing stone met the tunnel's softer floor. I kept digging with fingers and trowel, hoping to create a cavity under the huge stone from which he could slide free.

He's not going to die. He can't die …

I stopped and gasped as a pool of reddish-brown liquid bubbled up.

Oh, fuck. That's from his legs.

I couldn't dig anymore, or he'd bleed out. We'd have to keep the rest of the stones in place, wait for help, and hope it arrived before … I threw dirt back into the cavity and patted it hard, hoping to staunch the blood flow. That seemed to work.

I sat back, exhausted from my efforts, my breath ragged. I was only a kid. How was I supposed to save

Freddy on my own? Could we cut off the crushed part of his body like James Franco did in *127 Hours*? I didn't have a clue. Everything I knew about medical shit came from *Grey's Anatomy*. And that was mostly about sex in closets and code blue alerts and—

I grabbed my phone and woke it up. "Come on, come on …" I mumbled. "How many bars?"

I only saw two words, NO SERVICE.

"No!" I yelled. "No, no, no!"

There would be no 911 calls made, not here, not now.

Tears and sweat trailed off the end of my nose onto the rocks. I threw down the phone. "Fuck that stupid fucking Jimmy." I screamed, mouth wide open, spewing all the hate I had for the world in a torrent of obscenities. In that moment, I wanted to bring down the entire tunnel and damn us both.

With eyes swelling, I turned away to hide my shame for thinking so selfishly. There was nothing I could do now to keep Freddy alive. But I *could* keep him company through his last moments. That's what I'd want …

I sat cross-legged beside him, placed his head in my lap, held his hand, and stroked his smooth face. I lost track of time. "Fucking Jimmy …"

Freddy stirred, his arms shaking. "Stupid Jimmy," he mumbled between gasps of pain. "Musta been … methane pocket down there." He paused to catch his breath. "Never thought that stupid fuck would take me out with his own Darwin Award."

I cradled his head with both hands and bent over him, choking back tears.

He swayed in and out of consciousness. I had to keep him talking and awake. Something about body shock. And I was scared shitless of being left alone. So, I asked him to tell me a story. He chose a strange twisting series of stories about wizards, astronauts, skiers, Chinese grandfathers, theft, and murder, and they still haunt me to this day ...

A Visitor on a Rainy Night

by Karen Eisenbrey

After the last pot was scrubbed, Stell sent the evening's help home with a silver coin for her efforts and a cheerful, "Good night. Stay dry!" The clean plates were stacked, the mugs lined up, ready for the next day. Herbs steeped in a teapot for a soothing drink before bed.

The gentle patter of rain on the roof added to rather than detracted from the evening quiet. No travelers were spending the night at the Blue Heron, and the supper guests had departed soon after the last tale was told. Stell swept the pine floorboards, smooth with age and wear. The final task of the night before she relaxed with her tea. This was when she missed Crane the most. During the day, there was always work to distract her. In the evening, she was cooking and serving meals, and then telling stories. In the stillness after all that, she remembered how her son used to help clean up at the end of the night, the two of them sharing the work and talking over the day.

The local young people had stepped in admirably to assist her after Crane left town — how long ago now, a year? No, a year and a half. He'd left on his eighteenth birthday. No word in all that time. He was more like his father than she'd ever imagined. The old wizard never sent word ahead of his visits to Deep River. He wasn't truly old yet, but that was how he presented himself — Knot, she called him, for his weathered look and stubborn streak. He either liked to surprise her or didn't realize she might want to be prepared. She'd tried to bring Crane up better than that. Now she wasn't so sure she'd succeeded.

Stell smiled to herself. Maybe Knot would visit tonight. He had shown up the first time on a night like this; a rainy night in spring, when they were both about the age their son was now.

"... Crane!" a deep voice called from the wet darkness. The muffled cry repeated, but Stell couldn't understand more than her son's name. Knot? But he never came to the front door these days. His way was to fly through her bedroom window on owl's or eagle's wings. And he was too secretive to shout.

She unlatched the door and pulled it open. "Why are you shouting in the street at this hour? Crane isn't here, if-" Stell broke off and stared up at the towering figure. He wore a long cape and a wide, pointed hat, both woven of some fibrous material. The rain rolled off these garments and dripped to the ground.

"Are you the mamam of Crane?" the stranger asked, each word carefully enunciated.

"I ... yes, Crane is my son."

"But ... you are small like a child!"

Stell tried to imagine how she must look to this tall stranger. Crane had often teased her about her small stature once he grew past her. But none of her people had been big. There was no need to argue the point.

"I am Crane's mother, but he isn't here," she said firmly. She wouldn't show fear. "I don't know where he is."

"I do." The tall man glanced up at the dripping sky. His confident voice grew dejected and weary. "It is a wet night."

"Oh! I beg your pardon." Stell's resolve softened as any lingering fear fled. "Please come in where it's dry."

Yes, it was unwise to admit a stranger when she was alone at home. But he knew Crane. He knew where Crane was! It would be inhospitable to leave him outside in the rain. She ushered him in and pointed out pegs where he could hang his outer garments. Without the hat, he bore a superficial resemblance to Crane: about the same age; brown skin; long, dark hair; a lean build on a tall frame. He was at least a head taller than Crane, though, with a longer nose and darker eyes. He wore durable clothing made of deerhide, with a large carry bag slung over his shoulder.

"Why did you shout at the door instead of knocking?" Stell asked.

"We do not have solid doors like this," he said. "We ... call out."

"Who is 'we'? Are you —" Stell stopped herself from saying *a giant*. That was story talk. Possibly an insult. "Mountain Folk?" Still story talk, but more polite, she hoped.

He frowned. "Your people call us that. I am Aklaka."

"Then they are real," Stell whispered. She had heard that term from Crane or Knot, she couldn't remember which. *Aklaka* — the name the giants called themselves.

Stell had been telling stories about giants or Mountain Folk her whole life. In the stories, giants were monsters, Mountain Folk mysterious ... and maybe also monsters. Mythical beings who had disappeared from ordinary life in the distant past. Anyone who claimed to have seen Mountain Folk was met with skepticism at best. Stell had never imagined they would look like this. Like Crane. Like Knot. Like family.

"Who ... who are you?" Her voice trembled with a mix of fear and excitement. "How do you know Crane? Did he send you to me? Where is he?"

The young man smiled helplessly at the onslaught of questions. "My name is Chamokat. You may call me Moki." He glanced toward the fire. It had died down, but the embers still glowed. "May we sit?"

"Where are my manners? Yes, of course." Stell pulled a chair nearer the hearth for him and added wood to the dying fire. "I was about to have a hot drink. Would you like some?"

"Thank you. A hot drink is pleasant on such a night." Moki sighed as he took his seat. "I walked all day."

Stell poured the tea into two mugs and gave one to her guest. "You must be exhausted." She sat in her rocker.

Moki laughed softly. "It would have been better on a dry day, but I am used to traveling in all weather. But you want to know about Crane. I met him near the beginning of his first journey. The trees spoke to him, but he did not know how to Listen. That interested me, so I followed him and helped him when I could. I gave him a fish when he was out of food."

"Thank you for that," Stell said. "Are you a wizard, too?"

"I am a Listener. My people do not trust your wizard magic, though it also interests me."

"You speak our language well," Stell said. "I mean, I assume you have your own that's different. How did you learn?"

"Crane sought us out, after he had finished that first quest," Moki said. "We became good friends and learned from each other."

Stell frowned. "Your people don't trust wizards, but you welcomed one into your community?"

"Crane did not openly work his magic while he was with us," Moki explained. "You are correct — not all my people wanted him to stay. But my father trusted him, and his word has weight. Crane reminded him of an outsider he knew many years ago, before I was born. His *small friend.*" Moki chuckled at the nickname. "My father allowed him to serve as Aku's Keeper. Aku is our mountain."

"How ... interesting," Stell said. She knew Aku's name. "Have you met this man yourself?"

"No, but as far as I know, he still lives on the Mountain. I suppose I might meet him someday."

The back of Stell's neck prickled. Knot lived on the Mountain and had had some long ago contact with the Aklaka. But it appeared Crane had not seen fit to mention his father to his new friend. She forced a smile. "So Crane was with you long enough to teach you the Eukardian language?"

"We taught each other to speak, and he learned to Listen."

"He learned your language, too?" Stell didn't know what Moki meant by *listen*, but it seemed to be something more than hearing. Something beyond her, like magic. But she knew the power of language. She knew how a story worked. "Say something in your tongue, so I can hear what it sounds like."

Moki spoke, the consonants percussive, vowels pitched up and down like a song. Stell didn't understand a word except *Crane.*

"Like music!" she exclaimed. "What did you say?"

"Crane was with us until yesterday."

"What happened yesterday?" Stell braced herself for bad news. "Why are you here and he is not?"

"He has accepted a task that should have been mine." Moki gazed up into the shadows. "He goes in my place to an island from which none of my people has ever returned. It seemed only right I should bring you word."

She bowed her head and forced her voice to remain steady. "He is lost to me, then?"

He reached across and took her hand. "I do not believe Crane is lost. With his magic and what he has learned from us, he is better equipped to accomplish this task than any of my people. But ..."

"But what?" Stell asked. "You still have some doubt?"

"Nothing is assured. I think he will succeed." Moki squeezed her hand once more and released it. "But I have had a vision, a glimpse of the future sometimes given to Aklaka Listeners. I saw Crane with a small woman with bright hair. I think it means he will not return to my people afterward, but he may return to you, or another woman of your people. This is a guess — visions of the future are rarely clear."

Moki's confidence in Crane was encouraging. In his eyes, Stell's son was a capable man taking on a difficult task he was equipped to manage. Very different from the image she carried of a boy who didn't even believe in himself, who had set off on a quest before he felt ready.

"Why didn't he let me know all this himself?" Stell asked.

"He is traveling in the opposite direction, from wild country to wilder country," Moki said. "There is no easy way to send a message. And he didn't want to worry you."

"What did he think I would do with no word from him in a year and a half?" Stell drew a deep breath. "Worry is what mothers do."

Moki smiled. "Yes, ours too. I am sorry if I have given you more to worry about. I thought you should know. But also ... I wanted to meet the woman who raised a man of such courage and kindness. Crane is a brother to me. I wanted to know more of his people."

"Well, here I am" Stell spread her arms wide. "I wish I were more impressive."

"Enough for me," Moki said. "Crane says you tell stories. Will you tell one to me?"

"Any story, or something specific?" she asked. "I know hundreds of stories."

"Tell me ... the defining story of your people."

Stell sat back, at a loss for words. What was the defining story of her people, of Eukard? She smiled as it came to her. Yes, that one would do nicely. "I would be pleased to do that, Moki. Make yourself comfortable. It goes like this..."

Voices Carry

by Barb Lachenbruch

Gary insisted we stop for Thai food at a place we used to frequent back when we lived in Berkeley. "To power me through," he said. Because insisting was what his people did.

And even though I replied, "The kids will hate it," we went and had Thai all the same. Because going along quietly was what my people did. It didn't matter how much I'd tell him. Gary would see and hear the consequences soon enough.

As he settled the bill, Benjamin and Elspeth came out to the parked car to help me get the sleeping bags ready. A cool drizzle fell, the sort that excited me back when I was a Californian. But now we were returning to Oregon, and this rain would only make the drive more difficult.

The kids sat in the front seat while I did the work.

I lifted the hatchback, then tossed their travel bags up to them. "Change into your jammies. And brush your teeth."

"We're on a street," Elspeth said. "With a sidewalk. Did you notice?" She was eight.

"There's a steering wheel in my sternum," Benjamin, ten, grunted. "I'm starved."

"A deal's a deal," I said, unlatching both ends of the passenger seat. "We're driving all night, so you can sleep." With a touch, the seats flattened, making the back into a plane. "You can change in your bags. You'll eat your own food in the morning."

"Cheese pizza!" Benjamin crooned. "Extra-large. All for me."

"It'd burn your mouth, you wouldn't be able to talk," I said. "Careful what you wish for."

"Tomorrow's Y2K!" Elspeth cheered. "But how do we say it? *Twenty zero zero —*"

"No, it isn't," Benjamin said. "Tomorrow's New Year's Eve —"

"I thought New Year's Eve was the new year —"

"Do you even know what *eve* means?"

"Why should I? It's not like we go around saying *eve, eve, eve.*"

I opened the tailgate and paddled the sleeping bags toward me. The kids' bags slinked out of their stuff sacks like sighs. I unfurled them to the far left and far right, toes to the taillights, then stepped back. Cold rain wet my back.

The adult bag was as tight-packed as refrigerator cookie dough. In some macho burst, Gary had bought us an expedition bag. It was encased in extra-stiff blue Gore-Tex and extra-stuffed with uncrushable poly underneath and down above. Even though we took no expeditions, the bag made the ideal columnar barrier between the kids.

I sat, my calves against the wet bumper, and clasped its stuff sack between my thighs. Then I groped at the bag and pulled, grunting. Nothing moved. Then I tugged. Then I tugged again. Then finally, the expedition bag whooshed loose like a soundless birth.

Where had Gary been for all this?

I flung the giant tube between the kids' bags, tossed the pillows to their spots, and closed the tailgate. And there stood Gary, under the restaurant's eves.

"You ready yet?" he asked. That would have been funnier if he hadn't said the same thing in his parents' driveway after I'd returned from a last circuit for left-behind Christmas presents and socks. And I'd been the one to pack the suitcases, load the car. It wasn't my fault we'd left two hours late.

"I'll drive," I answered.

"No, I want to," he said.

"Swear you'll tell me if you're the least bit drowsy. We'll switch on the spot. Or I'll talk to keep you alert." I pulled my wet shirt loose from my back as I crossed to the passenger seat.

Gary reclined his seatback, then looked at me. "You ready yet?" he asked again.

"Kids? Are you settled?" I asked. They were still rustling.

"Kinda," Elspeth said.

"I'm hungry," Benjamin said.

"Sleep."

"It's barely 10 o'clock," Benjamin said.

"That's after your bedtime. We'll be home by 8:00 in the morning," I said. "The road vibes will make you sleepy."

"Not if I'm not sleepy." I saw his point, but I knew he was wrong.

"Happy New Year's Eve Eve," Elspeth sang.

Gary had already backed out. He pulled into the lane as I turned forward and snapped my belt shut. The ten-hour drive had begun.

On the freeway, I asked, "Do you have toll money out?"

Gary said nothing.

Unsure if he'd heard me, I said, "You'll need toll money. Do you have any handy? Or do you want me to get some out?"

No answer.

"No, I don't have any," I said for him, using his voice. "I'd like you to get it out for me, please. Oh, thank you. You anticipate my every need."

Even this got no response.

But when we got to the tollbooth, he reached his open hand for the dollar bills I clasped at my waist.

Off the bridge, I made sure we stayed on the correct freeway. An hour later, I alerted him to get in the right lane to change freeways again.

Traffic thinned, exits became less frequent, billboards more sparse. I checked his eyes, but they blinked normally: he was fully awake.

"I think Christmas went pretty well. It was fun seeing your family."

He said nothing.

"I like all the in-laws. That could be bad if I didn't, couldn't it? All the in-laws, having to be together so much. You brothers all know each other, but us wives, we have to be there." I spoke quietly because voices carry. But I was trying to get him to talk. That's what the passenger does; that was part of the deal.

Finally, he said, "I think I'll listen to the radio. Why don't you go to the back and get some sleep?"

"How about if I drive a couple hours?"

"No, I'm good," he said, so I sighed, unbuckled the seatbelt, and dove head-first over the console to the back.

Before I'd unfolded myself into the bag, I was blasted through by radio static from up front. The car jerked, and the volume settled down. After a few more jerks, the cocky voice of a male talk-show host came on, but over the wet-road noise, I could not make out the words.

I was not at all sleepy.

A half-hour later, he exited. For gas, I surmised, then confirmed when we came to a stop under daylight-bright lights.

The kids tossed.

"I'll drive now," I said.

"No, it's okay." The gas smell and cold slapped my senses when he left to fill the tank. I reached for my pink fleece, pulled it over me, and adjusted it so its appliquéd bears weren't poking my face.

The door opened. Gas. Cold. He was back.

I was fully alert. I should have been driving.

Nighttime was no stranger to me. I was always up with kids' ear infections, household chores, deadlines. And in bed, I was no stranger to the ruminations that took sleep's place. I would rock Gary gently and ask him for a take-off. *Garden hose,* he might spurt out, or *Scotchgard*, his list of topics for me queued and ready, without effort, like a woman's eggs. I'd try again if his offering sent me where I didn't want to be. *Mint toothpaste. Aluminum bleachers.* He'd be back asleep as I forced my mind to tell my head a story that would bear me off to sleep.

"Could I have a take-off?" I asked the front seat.

"*A blimp*. For if you don't want to drive."

This take-off was worthless—and the vibrations did no good, either. I could not sleep.

I finally told Gary, "I'm coming back over," and dove over the console again.

"For God's sake," he laughed as I worked to get myself head up and feet down.

"It's hard, this direction," I said. "God, we've only gone a hundred thirty miles? Let's talk. It's dull back there."

"What would we talk about?"

Technically, it had just turned New Year's Eve. "Tonight."

"What's tonight?"

"Gail and Rick's." The party at his work-friend's house.

"Do we have a sitter?"

"Yep, Cath."

"Do we have to bring anything?"

"We should. Wine. Little vegetable things—appetizers. We'll have to shop."

He said nothing.

"So, want to talk about it?" I asked.

"Tell you what. I'm pretty good just driving."

I'd never liked his driving. Only one hand gripped the wheel, and its thumb was curled in, at risk of being broken. His shoes, which he'd kicked off, lumbered in his footwell where they could creep underneath the pedals. He hadn't signaled his lane changes, and for one long minute, drove us in the blind spot of another car.

"Can I drive?" I finally asked.

"Wait 'til I'm sleepy."

"Promise you'll tell me," I said, but I could have been speaking to an airbag.

The rain let up, but minutes later, it started again. He'd been slow to turn off the wipers and now was slow to turn them on.

The freeway continued flat and straight. By now, he'd failed to dim his lights where the road wasn't divided and hadn't changed lanes for a merging truck. He'd driven on the noisy bumps between the lanes, and later, on the gravelly shoulder.

"You should be sleepy," I said.

"You sleep," he grumbled. "So later, you can drive."

I re-adjusted the fleece around my neck. I was seething: he was taking the entire easy shift for himself. Sometimes I almost wished I could do this whole drive without him.

I tried to sleep, but obligation would jerk me awake to check his eyes. Then I'd drift again.

But finally, the car slowed. The wheels were on gravel. We stopped. I sat up, alert. "Where are we?"

"Rest area. I'm going to close my eyes." He reclined his seat.

Three flagrant violations. He'd been driving sleepy, he hadn't asked me to keep him awake, and now, he parked his sleeping body in the driver's seat.

"I'll drive," I said. "But I'm going to pee first."

I got out, closing the door gently. We weren't at the rest area; we were on its offramp. He had been so sleepy he'd just pulled off.

Supporting myself with a hand on the door, I peed, then walked around the front, and got into the vacated driver's seat. After lobbing his shoes to the passenger side, I glanced in the mirror at the two flatter bags and the puffier expedition one in the middle. They rippled a bit. Gary had climbed over the console and laid down.

I started the engine, straightened the seatback, clicked my belt, and began the first leg of my drive. It was 1:22 a.m. Almost seven hours to go.

This was the hardest night-drive I'd ever done. Construction that closed lanes. Drowsiness that enveloped me. I considered the radio, but it would have awakened everyone—if there were even stations.

Gary should have offered support.

I opened my window, just a crack, to not wake anyone.

I opened my eyes wide.

I squinted them.

I contracted my glutes.

Did Kegels.

Kept driving.

Rain that intensified on the climb out of California. 3:00 a.m., the border. Oregon. Patches of fog. Narrow shoulders, barriers on the left. Slow-moving trucks that materialized only car-lengths away.

It was past time for Gary to make some offer, but he slept on.

5:00 in the morning. Three hours to go.

I'd tell myself a story. Not a short one to put me to sleep. A long, long interesting one—to keep me awake. *Seven keys*, I thought. *A prize that turns into a curse.* Dipping into another fog pocket, I tried another take-off, *Clouds that don't talk.*

As my foot, arms, and eyes drove the wagon, as Gary and the kids slept, my mind began to unreel the story to my head, a dramatic tale to keep me awake, a yarn full of murder and ghosts and the moon rising up over the highway…

Halftime

by Susan Hammerman

A dented metal table separated Lynne from the cop in the interrogation room. If Lynne had Googled "cop," she would have found a picture of this guy — buzz cut, mustache, big biceps, flabby stomach, clearly stupid.

He clicked his blue ballpoint pen twice. The legal pad in front of him was at least six pages in. The current page was nearly covered in block print. Significant words were underlined or had boxes drawn around them.

Lynne could make out a word here and there. 'Jolie, halftime, murder weapon.'

"Try again. From the beginning," he said.

Lynne forced herself to look up from the page. Relax. Make eye contact. Don't embellish. Answer questions with questions, and when cornered come out swinging.

"We started making the switch in fourth grade," Lynne said and flexed her wrists, so the handcuffs stopped biting into her skin. "We dressed alike, except her sweater was red, and mine was, whatever, yellow. Elaine was in loafers, and I had sneakers. Her hair was in braids, and I wore a headband. At lunch, in the bathroom, we traded cardigans and shoes. I braided my hair, and Elaine took hers down and got the headband."

The cop leaned back in his chair. It was obvious that he didn't believe her. "You and your sister have been doing this for thirty years and nobody figured it out? Not even your parents?"

"Well, not thirty years. I'm thirty-six," she said. "Where is Elaine? Is she in the next room getting interviewed by *your* brother?" Lynne laughed and shook her red tangled hair to get it out of her eyes.

"Okay. Elaine is your identical twin," he said.

"Can I have a glass of water?" Lynne asked. Her mouth was so dry.

"You don't want the Diet Coke?" He pointed at the can with his pen.

The fluorescent lights thrummed, and the sound made Lynne itch and want to move to get away from it.

"Describe what happened on Thursday," he said, all business.

Lynne drummed her sneakers on the tile floor.

He made eye contact and waited. His pen hovered a millimeter above the pad of paper, like he was willing her to say something else worth writing down.

They'd been through the story a dozen times. She'd memorized the words and recited them verbatim. "Every day is the same. We have keys to each other's apartments. We meet up at lunch, trade shoes and jackets, switch jewelry, whatever. Then she goes to my job, and I go to hers. Sometimes it lasts until the next day, and I stay at her place, and she stays in mine. I walk her dog, and Elaine feeds my fish. Got it now?"

"What time did you show up at her work that day?"

The room reeked of BO. It was the hot stench of sweat and dirty clothes. Lynne couldn't remember when she'd washed her t-shirt or her jeans or herself, for that matter.

"Which day?" Lynne asked.

"Thursday," he said and flipped back to the timeline he'd sketched on the first page. It started at eight in the morning and went to ten in the evening. Six twenty-five p.m. was underlined twice.

"After lunch, I guess."

"What did you do that morning?"

"Watched television." Lynne knew what his next three questions would be and answered them before he could ask. "I watched it all morning. I had the day off, and I don't remember."

"You don't remember what?"

"What I watched."

He added marks to the timeline and turned to a new page. "How do you know what to do at Elaine's job?"

Lynne shook her fists in exasperation. Her handcuffs rattled. "That's the fun of it. We need to figure it out. For something important we might leave a note, but we usually just know."

When they were kids, they had to clean their room and make their matching twin beds to get their allowance. Elaine knew she had to make Lynne's bed too. One time, after Elaine had made the beds and straightened up, Lynne had sneaked back into their bedroom and ripped the paisley comforter and lavender sheets off Elaine's bed and dumped them in the swimming pool in the backyard. No allowance that week.

"Tell me about Peter Hubert," the cop said.

Lynne didn't want to talk about Peter. She looked at her fingernails and saw blood. She'd been biting her nails again. "He's dating Elaine, not me."

"Is there take-off with him?"

"Halftime," Lynne said.

"Right. Is there 'halftime' with Peter? Do you do that?"

"No," Lynne said.

"What about Peter's wife?" he asked. "What can you tell me about her?"

"I didn't know he was married."

"But when you found her in the parking lot, you figured it out?"

"Yeah. Big knife. Blood all over the place. I managed to put two and two together."

More pen clicks were followed by, "How did you know who she was?"

Lynne plucked at the collar of her t-shirt. "I looked in her handbag. Her wallet."

He flipped back a page and underlined an entire sentence, put a box around another word, and drew an arrow to link the two together. He wrote 'fingerprints' in the margin.

"You didn't stick around to speak to the police after you made the call to report a body."

"Not sure what I could have done to help. I'm not a mortician."

Lynne opened the can of soda. She took a swallow and coughed up a metallic taste, the taste of chemicals. Diet Coke ran down her chin. She wiped it off on her sleeve and looked at the flecks of soda that mixed with the freckles on her arm. Kids in school teased her and called her Dippin Dots, because of the freckles that stood out on her pale skin, dotting her face and arms.

"Where was your sister when you found the body?"

"My place."

"How did you know that?"

"I called her," Lynne said.

"You called Elaine before you called the police? Can you explain why you did that?"

Lynne filled her mouth with soda and swished it around her teeth. Her tongue felt like sandpaper. She swallowed and said, "I was worried. Maybe Peter killed her, too."

"I'm confused. Now you're saying Peter murdered his wife?" he asked.

"Why not? Husbands kill their wives all the time."

"Her name was Jolie Hubert." He propped a tan elbow on the table. "Jolie *was* pretty. Was she prettier than your sister?"

"How would I know? She was a mess when I saw her. Sprawled out on the pavement."

He shuffled a couple of pages back and said, "That wasn't the first time you saw her, though. Right?"

Lynne slid down in her chair and closed her eyes. She pictured Jolie with her long brown hair. Dippin Dots had no chance against her.

Lynne kept her eyes squeezed shut. "I want to call my lawyer."

"You already called her. Do you want to keep talking or should we stop?"

"Whatever." Lynne righted herself in her chair and opened her eyes to find him scribbling away.

"What time did you and Elaine make the switch on Thursday? When was halftime?"

"We didn't. We were already dressed identically."

"Some days you didn't swap clothes? You planned in advance to dress the same?"

"Yeah," Lynne said.

"How did you know to go to the parking lot after you left Elaine's work? It's three blocks from your sister's office, and in the opposite direction of your apartment."

Someone knocked on the door.

The cop stood up and opened the door, but not wide enough for Lynne to see who it was.

"Detective Barns," the cop introduced himself through the doorway to the person standing in the hall.

"Would you like some time alone with your client?" he asked.

"Sorry?" a woman said from the hallway.

Lynne recognized the voice. Trickles of sweat skittered down her back.

"You're Lynne's attorney?" Detective Barns asked.

"What? No. I'm her sister. Lynne hasn't seen her lawyer yet?"

"Hold on," Detective Barns said. "You're Elaine?" he asked, astounded.

Another cop pushed the door open, peered at Lynne, and said, "She's in a suit and has a briefcase. She told me she was here to see Lynne Climpset. I thought she was the lawyer."

"Yeah, it usually helps to ask," Detective Barns said.

He turned back to Lynne. His eyes narrowed as he studied her, and his forehead scrunched up like a crumpled newspaper.

Lynne recognized that look that morphed from confused to judgmental. She'd seen it on the faces of teachers, employers, boyfriends, and strangers. There was a hard line between before and after. Before, she was treated like everyone else. Afterwards, she wasn't.

"Your identical twin is here to see you," Detective Barns said to Lynne.

Elaine maneuvered around the cop and stood in the doorway. She was as gorgeous as ever. Dressed in an expensive navy suit, she had a long purple scarf draped around her neck. Her perfectly straight black hair was cut to her chin, and her lipstick was cherry red.

"Don't worry, Lynne. It's going to be okay," Elaine said.

"You can't go in there," Detective Barns said and closed the door, leaving Lynne alone.

After several minutes, the cop came back into the room. "Elaine wanted me to give you this." He held up a black tube of lipstick. "She said it's your favorite."

The lipstick was a prize. Lynne bounced with excitement. "Ooohhh. Chanel! Take them off. Take them off." She rattled her handcuffs at him.

"You're going to stay in your seat this time?"

She plastered a grin on her face and said, "Of course."

He set the tube of lipstick on the table in front of her. He unlocked her handcuffs, took them off, and clipped them on his cop's tool belt.

Lynne dragged the red lipstick across her lips. It was luscious and smelled like roses.

He held out his hand.

"Wait," she said and felt along her right ear for her gold Scottie dog earring. She took it out. Their parents gave them a matching pair of gold Scottie dog earrings when they were ten years old. A week after they'd gotten them, when Lynne was brushing her teeth, she knocked hers down the drain. She was heartbroken. Elaine had taken out one of her earrings and given it to Lynne. From then on, they both wore just one.

"Tell Elaine that after twenty-six years, she can finally wear a matching set." Lynne placed the tube of lipstick and the gold earring on the cop's thick, meaty palm.

"You're sure? You don't want to speak to your lawyer? She asked to meet with you," Detective Barns said.

"She's Elaine's attorney, not mine," Lynne said. "Where is Elaine?"

"She's giving a voluntary statement about you." His voice was soft and steady. "I hate to tell you, Elaine's story and yours don't add up."

"No?"

"Elaine said she lends you clothes from time to time and confirmed that she has a key to your place. She also said you started showing up at her work unannounced, but Elaine said you don't swap jobs. There is no halftime, not since elementary school."

Lynne dragged her hand across her mouth. Red lipstick came off on her palm. She held up her hand and said, "Then explain this."

Detective Barns leaned forward to shorten the distance between them and said, "Elaine thought halftime, when you were kids, was to make her feel like you shared everything, when she was new to your family after her adoption. It wasn't to fool people. She said that you both were so unpopular in school that no one bothered to learn who was who – even the teachers didn't know. She wondered if that's the reason you're confused."

"I'm not confused," Lynne said.

Lynne could tell that he wanted to write on his pad of paper, but he didn't. She wanted to cry, but she didn't. If he could wait, she could too.

"Okay." He set his pen down. "I want to help you clear this up. Why don't you tell me what really happened to Jolie Hubert?"

"I found Jolie. I found the knife. I called the cops."

"Jolie was shot. Did Elaine put you up to calling the police?"

"No."

"You said you called Elaine on Thursday afternoon. You didn't. She called *you.* After that call, you called the police." He made a tent with his fat fingers and waited for her to respond.

"We talk to each other all the time. Twenty times a day. I can't keep track of which calls I made and which ones she made."

The cop leaned back in his chair. "I watched the security video from your building. Taken last Thursday. The video was of you, pacing back and forth on the sidewalk outside. I watched it on fast forward, because you were out there from two o'clock in the afternoon until eight at night. Which means, you were not in the parking lot, and you did not find Jolie's body."

Lynne studied the lipstick smear on her hand.

He said, "The parking lot doesn't have cameras, but Elaine's office building does. I also saw the video from your sister's work that shows her walking towards where Jolie's body was found, exactly twenty-five minutes before you called the police."

He finally stopped talking.

Lynne felt for her Scottie dog earring. "I gave it to Elaine. I forgot."

He said, "Did Elaine kill Jolie Hubert?"

Lynne whispered, "Of course not."

Detective Barns said, "As a cop, I hear all kinds of stories. Why don't I tell you a story, Lynne? Show you how it's done. Then, you can tell me a story. The one about what happened between six o'clock and six-thirty on Thursday. That's the story I need to hear."

Mama Only Visits When It's Dark

by Frances Lu-Pai Ippolito

A-gong watched his grandson, Xiao-yu, color rabbits picnicking in a cabbage patch. It was the fourth or fifth page that A-gong had watched the eight-year-old color. Each time, he colored the pages the same way—completely in black crayon. This last page in the book was no different. From the top to bottom, floppy ears, paws, cotton ball tails, the sky, and all the negative space in between, not a sliver of blank white remained. When he was done, the child dropped the crayon nub on the desk and pressed his face down into the page with his eyes wide open. Long, wispy eyelashes swept aside small pieces of crayon wax as he stared, unblinking into the black page.

A-gong wanted to pull Xiao-yu's head back by the hair, drag the boy outside, dress him in clean clothes, and force him to accept his mother's death.

Instead he said, "A-gong bang ni," and offered to bring Xiao-yu a new book from the little wooden shelf beside the desk. But when A-gong picked a coloring book and flipped it open, the page was already covered in black. He picked another page and then another. The result was the same—all the pages and all the books on the shelves were coated in black crayon, marker, or pencil lead.

"A-yu, you know you're not supposed to write on reading books," he said, holding up a picture book that once had a bright moon on the cover but now displayed a starless night.

"It's the only way." The child's voice was frail and hollow as if he were also made of paper like the books, an origami child, with no spine or bones to sustain him.

"The only way for what?"

"Mama only visits when it's dark."

"A-yu." A-gong stroked the boy's unwashed black hair and felt the oily clumps. "It's hard to accept."

The boy scowled and picked up the nub. "None of you believe me." He pressed the crayon against the desk and scribbled spirals across the bamboo surface for a minute or two before settling on a corner to fill.

"Let's get dressed. I'll take you fishing at your favorite lake."

"No." The crayoned mass grew over half the desk, forming dark clouds that spread over the tabletop like a menacing storm.

Joints cracked and popped when A-gong lowered himself down to one knee. Seventy is too old to take care of a child again, he thought as he brought his palm to Xiao-yu's cold cheek. The gray skin was papery and thin enough for A-gong to see the tangles and knots of blue-black veins underneath. The boy looked up. Dark half-moons under his eyes mirrored the circles he'd drawn on the table.

"Gong-gong, she's not dead."

"I miss her too."

The boy stiffened and moved his face away. "She's here." Xiao-yu pointed to the desk.

A-gong stared at the black shapes that veiled the desk's surface. Failing to see any particular forms or recognizable patterns, his gaze traveled down to Xiao-yu's bony arms and marker-stained fingers, and then to the dirty shirt that hung slack and oversized on his emaciated frame. The child smelled musty as well, like damp earth instead of flesh lived under the layer of frangible skin.

Cliff needs to take him to the doctor. Get him out of this room. A-gong knew his son-in-law was mourning—weren't they all? But something was not right with Xiao-yu. This was more than grieving.

"Can I draw with you?"

Xiao-yu nodded.

"I can teach you Chinese ink painting and calligraphy. My father taught me. I taught your mother when she was little."

The boy hesitated and studied the crayon in his fist. "Can we use black? Mama would like that."

A-gong nodded. "I'll get rice paper, brushes, and an ink stick."

Xiao-yu was smiling for once as he rubbed the tip of the ink stick on the stone saucer. Grinding with his whole arm, the stick abraded against the sloped stone sides and mixed with the water welling in the center of the dish.

"Gong-gong, how much water?"

"More water, lighter color," A-gong answered.

"Then no more. Mama only visits when it's dark."

The boy stood up from his chair and used both hands to push the stick back and forth until the ink was thick and opaque.

"Hold the brush like this." A-gong took Xiao-yu's hand in his and helped the boy position his fingers.

"Now, what would you like to paint?"

"Mama. I want to paint Mama."

A-gong frowned. Painting a person took years of practice. Rather than giving him a choice, he should have offered to teach Xiao-yu how to draw bamboo leaves first. Those were easiest for young, untrained hands.

"How about bamboo?"

"No! Mama!" the boy shrieked.

"Buyao shengqi." Don't get upset. A-gong patted his back. "I can teach you how to write 'Ma.'"

A-gong dipped the tip of his own brush into the ink dish, letting the thirsty hairs soak and drink their fill. He tapped the brush, raised it, and watched excess ink plop back into the disk. Next to the sitting boy, he glided the hairs across a white sheet of rice paper and formed the word "Mother" in Chinese.

"You try," he said to Xiao-yu.

Xiao-yu held his brush tight and pressed the tip into the paper. The brush whipped over the paper like a crayon. Ink bled and spread everywhere, expanding radially into black suns with spider-webbed rays. Frustrated, Xiao-yu zigged-zagged the brush left and right and tore a gash in the paper.

He threw the brush down onto the table, spraying droplets onto the cream bedroom wall behind the desk.

"I can't," the boy cried out and kicked the table legs, making the brush bounce and clatter up and down on the table.

A-gong gathered the boy into his arms and was surprised when his grandson let him. It was the first time since his daughter's death that Xiao-yu had allowed his grandfather to hold him like this. "Yes, you can. Your hands may not be strong enough right now, but you will be stronger, I promise."

"It's too hard." Xiao-yu sobbed into his grandfather's chest.

"Ssshh, we'll take a break and I'll tell you a story about finding the strength to make it home when you are lost." A-gong led Xiao-yu to the bed and helped him lay down. Sitting on the edge of the bed, A-gong patted away Xiao-yu's tears. *The boy is too light and clearly didn't eat or sleep enough, always coloring alone in his room.*

"I'll tell you the story, and when I'm finished, we can try again."

The boy wiped his eyes with his sleeves and cuddled closer to A-gong's knee. "Ok."

And A-gong began.

The Silk Road Leads to Iceland

by LM Zaerr

The shadows in the snow turned gray, and the light faded. "We should head back," said Bryn. "It's getting dark."

"One last run," Sara shouted over the wind. She twirled her ski poles and headed back up the slope with Connor beside her.

"We need to go now," said Bryn. They didn't hear. Bryn was a Classics professor, an expert on daring adventures, but she always had to be the sensible sibling. They were all grown up now, but she was still the oldest.. She clomped up the steep meadow toward Three Fingered Jack, fish boning where she could, sidestepping where she had to. She was out of breath when she caught up with the other two.

"Pergamobilia!" shouted Connor and took off. He always made up words and used them so vigorously they stuck, and Bryn found herself saying them outside the family and winning puzzled looks from friends.

Sara whooshed after him, laughing that musical laugh. She was out of sight before the wind swept away her voice.

Bryn squinted into the gray twilight. Tiny snowflakes pricked her face, her unprotected eyes. She pushed off. She was skiing blind. Her skinny Rossignols were too light for backcountry skiing, but she loved them. She could feel every swell, every clump of ice, the sheer sheets where rain had fallen on steep snow. Her anxiety turned to exhilaration. Her body balanced through every instability, for once free from her mind.

She snowplowed, turned, and stopped, gasping, by her brother and sister. "Time to go back," she said. "We can follow our tracks down to the Skyline Trail. I'll lead."

Bryn side-hilled, step by slow step, planting her poles, scanning the snow for their tracks. She found them, faint but still visible. She only realized how worried she'd been when her face and shoulders relaxed.

"Yay!" said Sara. "I've got tomato soup in a thermos in the car."

Bryn glided along the ski tracks, snowplowing through steeper pitches so she wouldn't move faster than her vision. The tracks were shallower than she remembered. The wind had blown new snow into the slots and pole marks. Then, abruptly, the tracks weren't there. "I've lost them," she called.

They spent valuable minutes crossing and recrossing the slope below until they finally gave up. "Never mind," said Connor. "We can sproodle to the snow park through the trees. I'll lead."

Bryn was glad to have someone else lead, and this way was faster, more direct. They'd done it before, threading around thickets and between trees, but always in daylight. The slope was more gradual than the Skyline Trail . . . if you found the right way. "Does anyone have a compass?" asked Bryn. "I have one on my phone, but it's in the car." She felt uncomfortable in the modern world and didn't like carrying her phone.

"Wouldn't work in this vivver anyway," said Connor, his voice as dim as his shape ahead. "I never bring my phone. Don't want it to broing some notification from work."

"You could silence it," said Bryn, annoyed with him because she was angry with herself. She should have brought her phone.

"I have mine," said Sara.

Connor stopped. "Better check the compass app. Just to be sure we're heading south."

Sara didn't even slip off her daypack. "The battery's dead."

"Then why did you bring it?" Bryn snapped, and immediately felt guilty. She hated being the grouchy one. She could pretend to be nice around other people, but somehow when she came home for the holidays she fell back into crankiness, especially when she was hungry. And she *was* hungry. They'd eaten all their lunch hours ago.

They kept going. The snow stopped, and the clouds cleared until they could see the moon through the trees, low in the sky.

"The moon is about to set," said Sara. Trust Sara to know about the moon. She was a musician, after all. "That means the moon is west. If we follow it, we'll hit the trail, and that will take us south to the car park. I'll lead."

"Yay for tomato soup," said Bryn, "and I brought Cambozola cheese and crackers for the car ride back."

They set off again, faster. Sara led them toward the moon until they came out of the woods on a high promontory. Bryn saw patches of stars above. She loved the constellations. They were all named for Greek and Roman stories. Below, a frozen lake glowed in the moonlight.

"Mosquito Lake," said Connor. "See those three stroops?" The *stroops* were the points at one end of the lake.

They cheered, and Bryn felt a release at the base of her ribcage. She knew where they were. Way off course, but from here it was only a mile to Highway 20, and they could follow the road back to their car.

They set off skiing again, trying to find a way down from the promontory. But tangles of brush forced them out of their way. They lost sight of the moon, and by the time they came out in a clearing the moon had set.

"Which way is south?" Sara asked in a small voice, a voice that made Bryn want to protect her, as she had when they were little.

Bryn looked up at the stars. She pointed with her ski pole, suddenly excited. "There's Orion's Belt. And his sword points south. I'll lead!"

"Yay!" shouted Sara.

"Nice going," said Connor.

As she skied, Bryn looked back and forth between Orion's sword and the dark woods. The contrast was disorienting. She edged around thickets, set her skis carefully between tree wells, and pushed past snow-laden branches. Sometimes she lurched unexpectedly, and once she lost her balance and her knee plunged deep into the snow. But she managed to lead them generally south.

The wind picked up. Clouds huddled back across the sky, blotting out patches of stars. Bryn stopped. As she watched, Orion disappeared. "He sheathed his sword," she said.

"Don't worry," said Connor. "Right now, we know which way is south, and it can't be far to the road. I'll head south in a straight line and stop. Then Sara can go past me and line herself up with Bryn and me. Then Bryn goes on and lines up with the two of us. Two points define a line, and our vector should stay steady enough to reach the road."

Trust him to come up with an engineer's solution. Hooray for engineers. They leapfrogged one round before the snow began to fall again. It filled the air between them. Bryn was at the back. It was her turn to move forward, but she couldn't see Connor. "Where are you?" she shouted. Only the sound of wind. "Connor!" She glided a step forward. "Connor! Sara!" She was alone. She hadn't realized how much comfort she'd drawn from the other two until they were gone. She was afraid to move, afraid any direction was wrong.

"This way," called Connor. She hurried toward his voice. Suddenly there he was, a few feet away, and Sara was standing next to him.

"We have to stay together or we'll lose each other," said Connor. "We'll just have to hope we're still heading south." He sounded hesitant.

"We can't go on," said Bryn. "We could ski off a cliff. One of us could break an arm or leg. Or worse."

"But we can't stop moving," said Sara. "We don't have enough clothes to stay warm. It's cold! Especially with that wind."

Bryn felt a shift, from merry adventure to survival. Her head and chest buzzed. She was frustrated, frantic. Then she realized. "I need food." They always listened when she said that. Not *I'm hungry*. When she ran out of food, she wasn't rational, couldn't make herself be.

"I've got a big bag of peanut M&M's," said Sara. "I'll open them for you." Bryn pushed down her anger at Sara's tact. Sara knew Bryn fumbled things when she needed food, and they needed every bit of food they had, couldn't drop M&M's into the darkness.

"We have to stay hydrated," said Connor in his most precise engineer voice. "I still have a full bottle."

"So do I," said Sara.

"Me, too," said Bryn. They'd each brought two. Her hands were shaking when she shrugged off her daypack. From cold? Needing food? Or fear? She pulled off a mitten and rummaged for her bottle but was afraid she'd spill it if she opened it now. She felt hard plastic. How could she have forgotten? "I've got a whole Tupperware of lebkuchen." She handed the box to Connor to open.

Connor gave her a diamond-shaped cookie, and Sara put five M&M's in her bare hand. A few minutes later, the frantic energy drained away. Bryn opened her water bottle and drank a few swallows.

"You gonna be OK?" asked Sara.

"Yeah. Peanuts work. And lebkuchen has enough real nutrition. Molasses . . . What does Mom put in there, anyway?"

"*Lebkuchen* means *life cookies* in German," chuckled Connor. "Appropriate."

"We're heroes," said Bryn, unaccountably cheerful. She intoned in her storytelling voice, "Sara brought understanding of the moon and the ways of intuition. I shared the lofty stars and the valor of the sword. Connor engineered a vector solution."

"And we all failed," said Connor.

"Now what?" asked Sara.

Bryn's mind was working again. "We make a labyrinth."

"Trust a Classic prof," laughed Sara. "You guys love labyrinths. Is there going to be a minotaur in it?"

"Look, it's logical," said Bryn, carried away with the idea. "We've got to keep moving, but it's not safe to wander blind. We'll make a track we can feel in the dark."

"I see," said Connor. "We make loops out and back, and then we ski around and around. That way we won't get farther from the road, and we won't amble off a cliff."

"All night," said Sara. "Mom and Dad will worry. We said we'd be back for a late dinner."

They were silent for a moment, worrying. "Nothing we can do about it," said Connor.

"I'll lead the way," said Bryn. It was very dark now, but she could make out the shapes of trees and bushes when she was close. She made a smooth curve out and back, trying to avoid crumbly snow near the trees, trying to avoid going through bushes. They seemed to be on a plateau. She heard the others rustling behind her. She half expected to ski on forever, so she was amazed when she crossed their track again. Connor struck out in another direction, making a new loop. Then Sara took over leading. Bryn was never sure where the new paths crossed the old ones. They forged a landscape of troughs until Bryn said, "Let's stop."

Sara murmured, "It's like polyphony, different melodies all at once."

"Or a program in C++," laughed Connor.

They plodded just fast enough to stay warm, naming the invisible landscape they had created. Five paths converged at Piccadilly Circus. From there, they could take Interstate 80 past Elsinore, a jumble of boulders as if a giant had dropped a ton of rock. If they paid attention, they could turn onto the Shambles, which looped into the woods on crumbly snow and exposed fir boughs. The Silk Road led to Iceland, where a tall tree sifted snow onto their heads and they broke through a skim of frozen rain. The Plain of Marathon offered a long, smooth stretch of trail with just one turn-off to the head-shaped rocks of Easter Island. They tried to avoid Fester City, which ran between two trees on unstable snow. Once they got to Aberystwyth, but they could never find it again.

The night stretched on and on. The wind died down, and it stopped snowing. They were slogging across the Plain of Marathon when Bryn heard a high squeal far away, repeated twice. "A whistle! They're looking for us."

"Mom and Dad must have gone to the snow park," said Connor. "When we didn't show up. Our car is there. They'll be looking for us."

"Like when we were kids," said Sara. "Parents don't stop wanting to rescue their kids."

Bryn longed for her parents and dreaded what they must be feeling.

They shouted and shouted, but the whistle didn't come again. "Maybe we imagined it," said Bryn.

They trudged on. Then Bryn heard Sara call from behind, "Where are you?"

"We're here," Bryn shouted. They all kept shouting until they met at Piccadilly Circus.

"I dozed off," Sara explained.

"Let's tell stories," said Connor. "You find truth in fiction, and we've got to do something to keep from slomping."

"Great idea," said Bryn. "Most stories are about survival. I'll start."

The slow swish of the skis set a rhythm for the story.

Shooting for the Moon

by Dr. Bunny McFadden

I looked down at my left leg and groaned. This was so embarrassing. A lady only gets to wear this fancy white getup once or twice in her life, and mine was stained with my blood. The folks who practically sewed my body into this getup would be pissed if they knew. If they were still alive. Nobody but Lupe Lucero would get shot on her way to the moon.

I pulled the lid of my helmet up and hunkered down next to the woman I'd been calling Valentina in my head. Each breath was endless suffering. We were crouching on the catwalk outside of the White Room, the motion-sensor elevator doors to the ground opening and shutting behind us. Below us, the Space Force airstream that drove us from our dorms to the rocket for launch day twanged as bullets flew back and forth.

"How am I doing, you ask? Oh, fine, just fine. Been shot by a deranged cowboy who thinks we're escaping this dying planet instead of trying one last time to save its sorry ass, but other than the gaping hole in my leg, I'm fine. How 'bout you, darlin'?"

Val was in a hurry, on account of the deranged cowboys, but she slowed to gently shift my body so that the folks on the ground couldn't shoot me again. I couldn't tell if she understood a word I said; she looked down at my leg with worry and ran her hand a few inches above it, as if she could wipe away the wound. I shivered. It was not our first intimate moment. There was an incident with salting a certain pumpkin soup in the astronaut dorms the other week. And another mixup when both of us tried to flip the hallway switch on the air-con in the middle of the night and our hands touched. These Houston nights get so hot you can't sleep. But the lady never spoke. I didn't even know her first name. The mission paperwork only used our last names. In my head, I called her Val, you know, after the first Soviet woman cosmonaut. Funny how badly I wanted to know her name before I bled out.

Since our rushed mission was getting so much bad press, the heads thought it would be smart to do some PR a few weeks ago. Two women, two astronauts about to save the world. Let's get a press shot of them with some school children. Don't get me wrong. Kids are fine. Just fine. I was one, myself, once upon a time. But god, they ask a lot of questions.

Most of them were teens who hadn't been drafted into the Space Force yet. There was this one, Maya, who was a smart little cuss. She told me personally that she'd be holding me accountable if the mission failed. Well, kiddo, if it fails, we're all dead anyway. And good ol' Val and I are the only ones who can launch Project Aegis.

"What do stars smell like?" one of them asked. I wanted to yell, "I don't know, Bobby. I ain't been to space yet!" I'd presume up there it smells like body odor and freeze dried food. Now I wondered if I'd get to smell it at all. Maybe it would just smell like rust from my blood.

Everything was going just fine. Sure, the mission was so rushed I never got the chance to meet my copilot formally, and anytime I asked for a translator, they told me we didn't need to talk much. We were both there for redundancy. One of us dies on the mission, the other can still finish the job. And Space Force also took my comms so I couldn't share my little updates with my family. What would I say anyway? "They fitted me for a helmet today. Boy, am I glad I have short hair! Makes the end of the world a little easier since I don't have to spend these last precious moments detangling." That sure would show Grandma that girls can, in fact, have short hair.

And they didn't let us watch the news. They probably didn't want us getting freaked out. But it was too late. Down there, at the entrance to the elevator that carries astronauts up to our doomed little rocket ship, there were three sharpshooting lunatics in an offroad vehicle. It had an upside down flag. It had a long banner. I couldn't read it. My eyes were blurry from the pain. But I knew what it probably said. "Project Moon is For The Loons." I hated that slogan. It was not Project Moon! It was Project Aegis. We were just launching it from the moon. But these anti-astro folks didn't know what they were talking about on the best of days. They were convinced we were leaving the planet and saving ourselves from the impending solar storm.

There were three of them at the start, but our security got the first two. I stopped trying to peek through the tiny slats in the steel grated floor and turned to look up at Val. If the folks downstairs knew I'd been shot, they would cancel the mission and then the whole planet was doomed. I pleaded with my eyes. Val, come through. Don't tell them. Just go in there without me. She seemed to understand. She turned to the little camera they had in the corner of the catwalk, right next to the elevator that brought us up, and aimed her gun.

For a moment, I was lost imagining running my hands through her pale hair. Val had a gun. Now where did she get a gun? We weren't supposed to bring any personal effects. I wasn't even allowed to wear my mom's lucky charm bracelet, the one with the little Dungeons and Dragons miniatures. And while I was over here bleeding and wondering how Val got a gun, she took out the final of the three deranged cowboys, hoisted me over her shoulder, and carried me over the threshold.

The White Room was built to filter eyebrow hairs and elbow dust. It threw a conniption when we brought blood in. In our handbook, it said we'd spend a little while here making sure we were clean and ready to load up and launch. I looked up at the clock. We were supposed to launch in twenty-three minutes. So she wasn't going to tell the folks downstairs. Was she going to leave me to bleed out in here? Of course not. Not good old Val. She simply shut the door, ran the air cycle, and then helped me limp into Lifty.

I rested for a moment in my seat, conscious that Ground Control was repeatedly buzzing.

"We're good," I said. I looked down at my leg. There was no way to know how bad the damage was. I'd been preparing to be an astronaut my whole life. I knew the inside of this rocket like a lemur knows his little cage at the zoo. I knew where to sit, which buttons ran which things. It made it a hell of a lot easier to lie.

The pain was urgent, like a bumblebee was stuck under my skin. I couldn't do it. I couldn't launch us. "Tell me a story," I begged her.

Sixty seconds until the rocket launched. All we had to do was hold on and press the right buttons.

Val cleared her throat and turned to me. After a moment, she nodded. "Yes, a story. I think it will help distract us."

In the Darkness and the Dunes

by Ann Ornie

I laid as still as I could, waiting for the others in the tent around me to fall asleep. I'd measured my breathing to be deep and steady. When my family's breath had matched my own, I'd opened my sleeping bag and deftly unzipped the tent's front flap.

When I'd passed well into the tree line, I turned on a small hand-held flashlight and moved the beam across the eerily still, pine forest. The trail was narrow and worn, but the white tennis shoes that had been awkward on my feet inside the sleeping bag were now appropriate and useful. They reflected the intermittent glow of the moon as it cut through the treetops, as if it was searching for me.

I shivered. The creepiness of the thought delighted me. A movement to my right caused me to turn. The beam, now erratic, caught the figure of my brother half blocked behind a tree.

I guess I hadn't been as stealthy as I'd hoped.

Bryce's eyes were wide as they reacted to the shock of the flashlight. I felt satisfaction at that. His pajamas and slippers were now dirty at the edges.

All at once, I hated him. I hated his ability to ruin my fun. But his ability to be so pathetic made me want to help him. That I hated more.

"Bryce, go back to camp." My voice was hard.

His eyes, still adjusting, stared past me. "I want to go with you." His bottom lip jutted out in determination.

"Well, you can't. Go back." I imagined my words pushing him back to the tent.

"No," he said stubbornly. "If you don't take me with you, I'll wake up Mom and Dad."

I weighed my options. I'd called his bluff once before, and he'd followed through.

"Fine. But keep quiet and stay out of my way." I tried to sound like it was my idea and not a forfeiture.

Bryce quickly crossed the dark to stand next to me.

"What are we doing?" he whispered.

"*WE* aren't doing anything. I am looking for aliens." He looked skyward, his bravery quickly ebbing away. "YOU are tagging along … as bait."

"I'm not bait!" he argued.

I felt a swelling of primitive delight in his fear. "You can tell that to the aliens when they beam you up. But I don't think they'll listen."

I moved further into the woods, passing through the cool rays of the moon that shimmered across the path like fairy lights.

I half expected him to turn back to the safety of the campsite, but he stayed close behind me, following within arm's length.

"What do you think space smells like?" Bryce whispered.

"I don't know... If you're there, it probably smells like fish food and farts."

"Nuh uh!" He whined.

"Be quiet or I'll turn around and go back to camp."

I heard him grumble and then fall into step behind me.

The trail wove through thick-trunked pine trees and opened at the crest of a large dune. During the day, children and families slid down the tangerine tinted sand, on plastic sleds, but at night, the wide treeless horizon allowed for an unobstructed view of the sky.

Once we were below the crest, I dug a shelf into the sand, creating a seat for Bryce and me to sit. There were no clouds in the sky. The full moon was set high with Mars and Saturn twinkling below her. They hung like candles in the window of space.

The sand still held heat from the day, but I suspected Bryce's pajamas wouldn't keep him warm for long. I couldn't let him go back alone without a light or without me. This set a timer to the night's adventure. Irritation blossomed in me. I took off my jacket and handed it to him to buy myself a few more precious minutes.

Try as I might to focus on the sky, I was very aware of Bryce, vigilant of any signs that he was getting cold, or tired, or scared. Maybe all three. But he was quiet and focused.

Around us the dunes were coming alive; the night creatures rose in a chorus of clicks and calls. After some adjustment, I pulled a small pair of binoculars from my sweatshirt pocket and took a short moment to focus on the moon. Its edges were textured and cratered. I knew it would be mean to not share this with Bryce and a part of me really wanted to be, but I shoved the binoculars to him and grunted. "Take a look."

He smiled, grabbed them and placed them on his eyes. His optimism annoyed me, but I was also proud of his interest.

We sat there for quite a while passing the binoculars back and forth. I pointed out stars and constellations. Each time, Bryce would listen patiently and then confirm my description for himself.

"You see that cluster of stars?" I asked. "That's Ursa Major, but most people call it the Big Dipper."

He nodded in acknowledgment.

"But," I said, my voice raising in excitement. "Ursa Major is actually a bear. See?" I pointed out the lighter stars that filled out the Big Dipper to become Ursa Major.

"What's the orange star?" he asked.

I looked up, curious. "Mars maybe? Show me which one." He handed me the binoculars.

"Just above the North Star," he said. "It's moving like a dragonfly."

I let my eyes relax and then focus out past the North Star. Sure enough, an orange light shone, insistent. It wasn't bright but glimmered as it moved side to side.

"Huh," I said, "I can see it … but I don't know what it is." *This was very promising!* It wasn't a planet, and it definitely wasn't a star that I was aware of. It didn't move like one either.

I felt Bryce sidle up closer, his teeth now chattering. *Just when it was getting good.* I focused harder trying to understand what I was seeing. Cheap binoculars weren't meant to be used on real life moving targets … I was sure there was a shape behind the gleam, something solid that was moving too quickly side to side and too quietly to be any airplane I'd seen before. As I leaned forward while struggling with the binocular's dials, a bright light washed out my vision.

"Bryce!" I hissed, "Don't do that!"

"It wasn't me," he said. His voice was a whisper from my left.

"The dunes are closed at night," an authoritative voice said from behind the beam. A large brimmed hat of a uniform was silhouetted by the moon.

I froze. Of all the scenarios I'd imagined for my adventure, being caught by a ranger wasn't one of them.

"Where are your parents?"

"Th-they just left," I heard Bryce say, "We are supposed to follow them."

"The dunes are no place for kids at night."

"We were star gazing," I offered, hoping that such an innocent detail would smooth over our trespass.

"It is a dangerous place," the voice said.

"He's just trying to scare us," I whispered to Bryce.

"Strange things happen here in the dark."

"What sort of things?" Bryce asked. There was a quiver in his voice that matched the floating sensation in my stomach.

The ranger bent down toward us, his hat blocking out the moon, and said, "Let me share a story of another young woman that reminds me of you."

A gold badge with four bold letters, "KUHL" flashed as it caught the light of the ranger's flashlight.

"Sometimes," he began, "taking a risk or a dare can be a fun thing..."

The Noir Side of the Pinot

by Debby Dodds

Soon I'd be able to quit, and I'd never again have to watch the dark red liquid fill the seemingly never-ending glasses in front of me. My job made me feel as if I was in one of Dante's levels of purgatory. I longed for the day I'd never have to see these drinkers and their smug douchecanoe faces again, the unmitigated joy of having enough money to not have to listen to their inane prattling.

"I taste a chocolate note more than the tobacco hint I'd expected…"

"Really? Because my palate senses clove and raspberry front notes…"

Sometimes as I stood there, a smile plastered on my waxy, lipstick-covered lips (I'd been told by the manager that lipstick made me more "approachable"), something unusual would happen: The tasters would remember I was there.

"Stephanie, what do you think of this vintage?"

"Oh, my palate is still developing, but I've heard the viticulturist refer to the nose as burnt toast." It didn't matter what I said, what silly thing I made up, as long as I pretended it was what the *winemaker* said it smelled or tasted like: pencil lead, wet wool, ashes, blood, etc. These sheep would nod and agree.

These "members"—who paid triple or quadruple the highest Costco price of a bottle of wine to have the tasting experience at the winery—felt all classy because they were getting day drunk "for free." Of all the jobs I'd had, from waitressing at a popular brick oven pizza joint to spraying perfume on crusty women at an upscale department store, this was the worst.

I'd been an art major at a state college on the East Coast. I'd never done anything in my life even remotely related to all the courses I took in school. But, somehow, I still owed over $50,000 on loans for my tuition. I'd ended up in Los Angeles following my college sweetheart who wanted to be an actress. She was now married to a famous director and had three kids and a Vicodin addiction. After we'd split, I'd meandered up to Northern California like an untethered row boat drifts out to sea.

Each day I came to work, I felt the bitter tang of derision that I've come to expect as my beat-up Subaru rounded the tree-lined bend to the dirt road, past the pond, past the vineyard, and past the giant castle-like main house, to arrive at the Domaine Riche tasting room decorated to look like some 17th-century monastery.

How many times had I wanted to shove a corkscrew through the vulnerable, gulping larynx of a guest? All while I tilted my head coyly, pretending to be fascinated by the blathering.

Honestly, I was doing them all a favor by plotting my caper.

It would be easy, really, to steal the $450,000 bottle of 1992 Hungry Coyote from the vault downstairs. I had keys to every door and was trusted to lock up most evenings. The owner of the winery was always traveling. And the general manager was having an affair with one of the married migrant workers, so he was all about leaving early before we closed.

A year ago, when I started working at the winery, I'd asked why that particular year and vintage was so expensive. I'd been told that not only was the vintage "unfiltered, undefined and rare because of its low production," but it had also been accidentally stored in a crawl space with no exposure to light. A single bottle had gone for more than a half a million at an auction, and we were down to only seven bottles left.

I had a buyer all set up. Or rather he had me set up.

Normally, Mr. Kuhl came in about once a month, had a few sips of the new releases, then left. He tipped well and was unfailingly polite. He never tried to make small talk and seemed to genuinely appreciate the wine with his discerning palate. He watched everyone around him intently. Once I watched him, as he watched a gorgeous redhead slip some money out of her older male companion's wallet while he stumbled off to the bathroom. I wondered: Would Mr. Kuhl tip the guy off? Laugh? Be impressed by the woman?

He did none of those things. His face remained inscrutable. Instead, he turned to look at me. *To read my reaction?*

Mr. Kuhl had the kind of spray-tan that looked more like he'd gotten a nasty sunburn at Burning Man than from what I assume was his goal, that of a dilettante who'd been lazing on a yacht in the Mediterranean. His bushy eyebrows arched up at their tails, giving him the look of someone always about to crack wise. Yet he was soft-spoken and serious every time I'd talked to him.

One day we were alone in one of the V.I.P. rooms. "You have something that I very much want," he said, settling back onto his violet couch.

Did his tongue flick out and lick his lips, or did I just imagine that?

"Could I corrupt you?" My stomach twisted on itself like a cheap chain necklace that you can't untangle without breaking. I expected some kind of sexual advance but none was forthcoming. Taking advantage of my silence, he looked deeply into my eyes. "Could you steal something for me?'

"Maybe I could, but I wouldn't." My hand gripped the bottle I held, tighter. "I'm no thief."

"Of course not," he said. And that was it. He didn't push. And, for his next few visits, didn't bring it up again.

I'm not sure why I didn't tell anyone what he said. Not even my new girlfriend Luna who sold hand-beaded necklaces at Saturday market and was always down to trade funny and irritating stories from work.

That summer, as the wildfires ripped through the eastern part of the state and we were facing a record heatwave, Luna announced she was leaving me to move to Seattle. She completely gave up on both me and our cat Bum Bum who was dying of cancer. Poor Bum Bum passed away only two months after she abandoned us. I was heartbroken. Then my only friend Danny moved to Hawaii after selling his car.

Time crawled by. Day in and day out, the people I had to pour wine for got worse. It had always been an odd mishmash of deranged cowboys, women dressing to look like identical twins, spouses who barely hid their disdain for each other, and snow bunnies and powder hounds enjoying their après-ski. They spoke of the nuisance of the homeless, the diseases of immigrants, and the fakeness of the news. Even the "liberals" could barely hide their disdain for the "workers trying to live off the government" who refused to do their gardening, childcare, and housekeeping.

Then on the first day of fall, Mr. Kuhl showed up at 10 am, right as the winery opened. That had never happened before. He was not usually impatient or hurried. He took up from where we left off that day of his offer, as though the three months hadn't passed at all. "And I wouldn't ask again but, well, I think it might be fun for you. It might be what you need to break out of the rut you are in." He smiled impishly.

"Okay, well, you have my attention now anyway." I set the bottle of Cabernet that I'd just decanted down on the table. I knew I didn't have long before the bachelorette party that had rented the red room would show up.

"It's just one little bottle of wine you need to take." I knew immediately what he wanted: The Hungry Coyote. He methodically yet efficiently laid out his plan for me to steal the bottle and deliver it to him.

The proposition struck me as odd. I'd heard through winery gossip that Mr. Kuhl lived in a multimillion-dollar penthouse apartment, and I'd seen his Tesla. It seemed like he could buy the bottle if he really wanted it. But then again, who was I to talk? I certainly knew you couldn't live your life on credit cards and debt. I looked like I could afford a sandwich from Subway for lunch but, really, I was putting that Turkey BMT on one of my Visas.

His face softened and he leaned forward a bit, "If you could do this for me, I'll make sure you're taken care of." At that moment, he struck me as more earnest than almost anyone I knew.

I could take the cash and disappear. My foster parents didn't keep in touch; they had other younger, more pliable kids to worry about. I'd cut them out of my life years ago. I had nobody and nothing keeping me here. I'd reinvent myself in Mexico. Mr. Kuhl promised he had a friend who could give me a new ID as part of the deal without even touching my $400,000.

Did it bother me that he seemed to be making very little profit on the resale of the bottle, or, if he was drinking the wine himself, saving very little money not buying it directly? No. I'd learned long ago to stop caring about the motives or happiness of other people because they didn't care about me.

I left the room after making the deal and made a beeline to the kitchen to see what the caterer was making for tasting pairings tonight at the monthly club dinner. It was Swiss chard with garlic and short ribs on a tiny croissant, little Pad Thai plates with lobster instead of chicken, and tiny ramekins of molten dark chocolate with a raspberry on top.

Weird. I'd been expecting deviled eggs because I'd smelled an almost sulfuric scent when I'd been with Mr. Kuhl.

The week before the whole thing was scheduled to go down, I had the most bizarre dream.

Some owl-like thing had me on a pedestal above a bunch of other people below who were swimming in a cesspool with fishes that had pig faces. Some tinkling music was playing off in the distance on a verdant hill, and life-like figs were dancing jigs. Then the Owl started clapping, and the crows above started crapping on our heads. But instead of that white guano that usually comes out, it was liquid gold. It burned the skin on my arm. I started panicking, worried that the owl creature was going to devour me now that he saw my bones. A robot, shaped like a dachshund, warned me to "Get out NOW!"

I woke up covered in sweat wondering what I'd consumed the night before to cause this Hieronymus Bosch dream of epic proportions. *Maybe I had a fever?* I felt my forehead, and it was cold and clammy. I shook it off.

The afternoon before the heist-day, a new man stood in the tasting room. Small and thin, he wore white pants and a blue shirt. At first, I thought he was elderly when he had his back to me, but when I approached, he turned, and he had an unlined face and thick blond hair under his cap. He stood out to me because he'd come in a half hour before I was going to close. He told me he'd be no trouble, that he only wanted a small flight. I nodded and told him that'd be no problem. But I was suspicious of him, so I looked his name up on our membership list: Angelo Custode. This surprised me because I'd totally expected him to not be on it, but he was. And even more confusing, his "join" date was the same year as the winery opened. I'd been sure I knew all the OG members from the various parties and events.

I almost drifted off when he started to tell me his story, anticipating boredom. It wasn't the first time a guy had started to confess his sins to me as I was pouring for him. Tasting room hosts are the new priests. But this time was different. Mr. Custode wanted to tell me not about himself, but someone else. Someone who was suffering more than I was.

I listened, and it changed me.

Visiting Hours

by Gabby Gilliam

The hospital room was never silent. The heart monitor beeped out the rhythm of Ryan's pulse. A steady hiss of oxygen escaped the cannula in his nose. Orthopedic shoes squeaked in the hallway outside the door. The curtain rattled when the nurse pulled it aside to check Ryan's vitals. Once she recorded the numbers on her tablet, the door clicked softly shut behind her.

A few minutes passed in the sterile, not quite silence before Ryan's door eased back open. His mother's feet ghosted over the sheet-tiled floor. The lights in Ryan's room were kept dim to maintain the illusion that he was just napping. The partial darkness masked the dark circles under her eyes, the chapped skin of her nose and eyelids. She wore the same sweatpants she had worn the day before, but the staff overlooked it. Her hooded sweatshirt had a hole in the left pocket, and her car key poked through. Her thin brown hair had grown noticeably more gray in the past two months. She no longer took the time to disguise it with dye. She had it pulled back in a sloppy bun. She hadn't run a brush through it in days.

She set her tote bag in the chair near his bed and reached out to take his hand. She bent over and brushed her lips across his forehead in a series of featherlight kisses.

"Hi Ryan," she breathed into his hair. "It's Mama." Ryan didn't respond. He never did, but she talked to him every day anyway.

His fingers were cool against hers, his skin dry from the stale hospital air. She pulled a bottle of lotion from her bag and began to massage it into his hands, taking extra care to moisten the thin skin between his fingers. She hummed as she worked, the notes of Baby Mine blending with the hospital hisses and beeps. Dumbo had been Ryan's favorite movie when he was three. He would sometimes ask to watch it twice in one day. Elephants were still his favorite animal.

Her practiced strokes matched the tune's melody, smooth and gentle. She worked lotion into his arms, then covered them with the scratchy hospital blanket. She had asked to bring Ryan a blanket from home, but the staff had refused, claiming they couldn't launder it with the rest of the linens, and it wouldn't be sanitary. Ryan's mother pulled the blanket from his feet and lower legs, rubbing lotion in as she worked her way up to his knees. Then she pulled his hospital gown, and the blanket back into place.

Ryan looked smaller in the hospital bed, sleeping among his wires and tubes. She brushed his hair across his forehead. It had grown long enough that it would have poked him in the eyes had he ever opened them. The hospital light made the dirty blond strands look as washed out and pale as the rest of him. With every day he spent there, it seemed as though he shrank a little more, flesh melting from bone into the stiff mattress beneath him.

"I picked up a new book from the library for you," she said softly. "I thought we could read some of it together."

She had already finished three books since he had been admitted to the hospital. The first had been a short chapter book that only took three visits from cover to cover. She had hoped he would be awake by the end, foolishly believing he would get better and she could take him home to their sofa and his video games. As the days turned into weeks, she had reluctantly brought longer books. She read until her voice grew hoarse, wanting to fill the room with more than just the sounds of machines. She wanted Ryan to hear that she was there with him, wanted the first sound he heard to be the sound of her voice.

She pulled a battered hardcover book from her tote bag before moving the bag to the floor so she could sit in the chair.

"It's a collection of science fiction stories," she told him. "The librarian said the one where the kids get caught when they sneak out to look for aliens was one of her son's favorites."

She flipped to the first page and began to read.

Storytellers
(continued)

by Benjamin Gorman

The night was getting cold, and cold is harder on old joints than young ones, so I was really feeling it in my knees at that point. I could have turned up the fire, but if it had been hot enough to keep me warm, it would have burned my kneecaps. Plus, the folding chairs don't have any kind of insulation, so my ass was freezing. I groaned as I leaned forward and picked up my thermos. I don't need to groan when I bend forward. I'm only 244 for 'roidssake. But I find I like to groan when I move. I have since I was middle aged. Back then, it was something of a dad joke, making fun of myself for being old. Joke's on me, now. It's become such a habit, I sound like I'm 300, and it makes young people think I'm that much older. They're no good at judging the ages of people who've been around for more than two hundred years, anyway.

'Course, I couldn't judge Zora by how old she looked, either. I can hardly keep track of how old she is. My years? Hers? I don't know either one. She looked like she was maybe thirty, but she must have been born almost a hundred years ago, Luyten b time. 'Cause, if I remember correctly, Rosey was around sixty when she had her, and she was in her mid-150s, so ... But I'm getting distracted with math. Anyway, I was freezing my ass off there on the cliff with Zora. I took a big swig of coffee to try and warm up.

"So, you can see where I'm going with this, right?"

She frowned. "Nesting dolls?"

"Right. One inside the other."

I sat back heavily, making the folding chair creak and the legs grind a little on the rocks. But I didn't groan. Not that time. My obvious self-satisfaction was bait. I wanted the silence to do some work.

"Okay, but ..." Zora said.

"But?" I asked. I'm sure she could see my smile in the moonlight. I couldn't hide it in my voice.

"But they're all wrong. Your nesting doll is all messed up, Grandpa. I guess ..." Now it was her turn to sit back heavily. "I guess I just don't get it."

"But why not? Think about it. People are in a story. And inside that story, someone tells a story. What's wrong with it?" I carefully didn't ask, "What's wrong with *that*?" I wanted her to answer. About the story as a whole.

"Each one is incomplete. Broken. They just stop when someone is telling a story."

"But couldn't that be right, Zora? Doesn't that happen in the universe all the time? A ship hits a rock that hadn't been mapped and blows up, just disappears in transit. A cave collapses. A child loses a mother. A father loses a daughter. A kid in a coma just stays in a coma. Someone decides to throw her life away by stealing from work. Some siblings sneak out of camp and get caught. Others get lost and freeze to death. Somebody kills someone else for no asteroiding reason at all. Somebody wakes up and decides their marriage is over. Somebody meets the love of her life and gets shot before she can tell her. Someone tries to find just what she needs, and it's not there. Someone tries to understand a new group of people, and they make no sense to him. Somebody talks your ear off in a bar, then decides she doesn't like you, pays her tab, and walks away. Those things happen all the time, right?"

"But not in stories. They come to an end."

"Because if they don't ..."

"Because if they don't, they feel wrong."

"Right," I said. "Exactly so. We know that the universe is not always right because it doesn't work like our stories. Outside the snake, it's chaos. Shit just happens. But inside, the stories work properly. And it is so much work, isn't it, Zora? We gnaw on our own tails, not just every once in a while, but all the time, trying and failing and trying again, to shape the worlds, our worlds, our lives, into stories that make sense."

I'm honestly not sure if I told her this because I'd decided she was old enough to understand, or if I'd decided I was old enough that I had to get it out before I couldn't anymore. Sure, I have lots of time left, but the years when she's gone get longer and longer. One day she'll wake up out of one of her travel sleeps, check her mail, and read that I'm dead. Morbid to contemplate, but it's going to happen. Bound to. And by the time she gets back, they'll have had my service and buried me in a grave right out here by the cliffside, and she can come out here with her parents and have a drink and maybe watch the moons rise, but I'll be gone. She will have all my love for her, and she'll have her memories of our times like this one, but I want her to have this story. I want it to be complete. I want the story to be right. Maybe that's just vanity. I used to think so. I thought our urge to be remembered was stupid, frankly. Pointless. And I was angry about that, bitter, mad at myself for feeling this thing I didn't want to feel. But I don't think so anymore. I've come to believe it's important. It's not just about some piece of me living on. It's something I can give her which may help her later. It may get her through. Or maybe, if she shares it, it will get someone else through.

I took another gulp of the coffee, felt it warm my throat, my chest, my belly. "You're right, Zora. It's not finished. Not by a longshot. Just a little space between the snake's tail and its fangs. Just a half a blank page. Because it can't end here."

I reached over and took her hand. Warmer than mine, even in the same cold air. I squeezed. I wanted her to feel how important this was to me, that little twitch in the old muscles in my wrinkled up old hands, my blood still pumping hard though both our veins.

"It can't. We can't let it."

Visiting Hours

(continued)

by Gabby Gilliam

Her voice cracked on the last word, her throat parched. Maybe Zora and her grandfather's story wouldn't end there, but it would have to for now. Her voice wouldn't make it through even another page. She pulled a bottle of water from her bag and took long, greedy gulps. She stared at the ceiling tiles as she drank, trying not to let her despair rise to the surface. She knew from experience that once she began to cry, it would be a long time before she could pull herself back together.

Ryan's fingers twitched, but his mother was too busy blinking away tears to see it. She tucked the bottle of water back into her bag, followed by the book. She reached out and squeezed Ryan's hand. He didn't squeeze back. She had stopped expecting him to. She stood with a sigh and leaned down to give him another kiss on the forehead.

"I'm going to run and get a bite to eat," she whispered to him. "I'll be back soon, ok?"

The only reply was the hiss of the cannula and the beeps of the monitors.

She turned at the door for one last look before she left for dinner.

"I love you," she said to the sleeping boy on the bed. When his fingers twitched a second time, she was already gone.

The Noir Side of the Pinot
(continued)

by Debby Dodds

I hadn't cried in so long that, after I heard the story of that poor mother, it was like a cork popped in me. I'd been feeling so cheated by life, so bitter, and I'd bottle up my sadness until it fermented and turned into a vinegary-bitter anger. But now I realized so many people had suffered things much worse than what I had.

As I wept, Angelo Custode took my hands in his. "When you can still have empathy and compassion for others, you can still find joy in the world." Angelo seemed to glow like he'd swallowed a moon. Or even four moons.

After that, I decided to decline my big payday with Mr. Kuhl. I texted him my decision and he only texted back in angry caps: FREE WILL. YOUR CHOICE.

I did change after that. I turned in my resignation. There were so many other jobs, so many other possibilities. Why had I seen life as narrow when it was, in reality, so expansive? The weird thing was that Mr. Kuhl disappeared. He was someone I was glad I didn't make a deal with. I worried for others that might make a bargain with him because he reminded me of a hungry mosquito that wouldn't ever stop sucking you dry once he got his stinger into you. But he never tried to contact me again. It seemed he'd evaporated like the smoke from a small ground spinner firework.

My last day at Domaine Riche, I walked out of the tasting room, breathing deeply, catching the scent of opportunity. The winery dog owned by the GM came up and licked my hand before trotting off to his kennel.

I had a wonderful life, and I was excited for it all.

In the Darkness and the Dunes
(continued)

by Ann Ornie

A deep chill had settled onto the dunes. The sand that had been warm was now cold against the back of my legs, and I could see that Bryce was shivering. I had already given him my jacket. There wasn't much else I could do to keep him warm.

We'd definitely been out here too long. Guilt pulled at me. I should have noticed sooner.

"I suggest you get a move on," Ranger Kuhl said, his face still hidden behind the light. "And I better not see you back here again."

"Y-y-yes sir," I stammered. I jumped up, grabbed Bryce by the back of the jacket, and scrambled over the ridge and into the trees, pulling him behind me.

"Marilynn ..." Bryce whispered when we'd gotten free of the flashlight beam that had followed us well into the woods. "Are we going to be in trouble?"

"I don't know," I admitted, looking back over my shoulder to the darkness behind us. The moonlight didn't illuminate our way anymore as the trees leaned over our heads hiding us from the sky. We slipped between the last pines into the campground to the safety of our parents that pulled at us like a beacon. Neither of them stirred as we silently undid the zipper of the tent and shimmied into cold sleeping bags. Between our mother and father's gentle snores, I listened for footsteps of the ranger. Bryce was also still awake. I could see the whites of his eyes glowing in the murky haze inside the tent. Every sound outside made the space between my shoulders tighten with anxiety.

When dawn finally warmed the top of the tent in a safe golden hue, I allowed my heavy lids to close.

Confused, our parents asked why we were both such sleepy heads.

"I didn't sleep so good," admitted Bryce between mouthfuls of cereal. "I kept waking up."

"Really?" our father asked in surprise, "I slept like a baby!"

Our mother agreed. "Best sleep I've had in ages."

I breathed a silent sigh of relief, thankful that they hadn't caught on to our midnight adventure.

Throughout the day, exhaustion tugged at us. Neither of us were excited to go to the park's dinosaur museum, despite our nagging the day before. We moved like sloths between each stop along the scenic route through the park.

"You poor things," our mother said as she lovingly patted Bryce on the head.

"I'm sure we'll sleep better tonight," I offered, but I knew I wouldn't be able to sleep as long as we were here. The memory of the shape in the sky and the ranger's story played like a reel in my mind, Ranger Kuhl had spoken as if life was narrow when it was, in reality, so expansive, and I feared what would happen when I fell asleep.

That night, Bryce and I laid awake inside our sleeping bags. We listened with dread for anything that could possibly be the footfalls of the ranger's boots, as the wind moved the trees around our campsite. Campers in the distance settled into their tents and trailers, while camp fires that crackled warmly died down. People laughing in the distance eventually became still until there was only silence and the wide expanse of the open sky above the dunes, waiting for us to close our eyes.

Shooting for the Moon
(continued)

by Dr. Bunny McFadden

I couldn't believe it. This was the first time I'd ever heard Valentina's voice. It was gravelly but rich, like the silt at the bottom of the river I used to play in as a kid. I felt myself unspooling as she told me her story. I didn't really understand what she said, but it got me through the worst of the launch. We were in orbit eight-and-a-half minutes later.

By the end of it, we were among the stars, and I was sure of one thing. I was going to live, we were going to make it back to Earth, and when we got there,

I was going to marry this cosmonaut. You can't get that close to the moon with someone and not fall a little in love. I spent the whole time leading to our launch building Valentina up like a character, brick by brick, and the real thing was even better.

We had six more hours to get to the space station, and then we'd head to the moon and put the final touches on Project Aegis.

Val unbuckled briefly to lean over and rip the cuff of my stupid suit off. Damn. We'd spent about an hour in the Suit Up Room getting these bad boys through their final checks, and now here I was with my bare leg hanging out, little drops of ruby blood like jewels floating in space.

"It's just grazed."

"Oh, I was wondering if you were going to say anything else," I teased.

She inspected me as I tried to respond to Ground Control. It felt scandalous.

"No abnormalities to report," I said as I hurried to shut off the mic.

Val was using a wipe to clean the wound.

"Oh, my," I joked as I gritted my teeth. "You've seen my ankles. That means we're basically married now."

She didn't say a word. Not that I expected her to. Val didn't even sing in the shower or hum when she cooked us pancakes on the weekends we didn't have training. Her hands were mesmerizing. The way she cracked eggs was heaven.

She wrapped my leg three times and patted me softly.

Maybe it was the shock, but that's how the stars smelled. Like what the love of your life cooks on the weekends.

The Silk Road Leads to Iceland
(continued)

by LM Zaerr

"So the astronaut loved Val even before she heard her speak," said Connor as Bryn ended her story.

All that long midwinter night, Bryn had skied through the snow labyrinth with her brother and sister, telling stories of survival. The stars had come out, casting a silver sheen, not enough to see beyond their track. The gaiters their mother had made kept the snow off their socks, though Bryn felt chilly damp leaking into the boots she'd had since high school. They took turns telling the stories and their stories wove in and out of each other like the labyrinth.

The lebkuchen and peanut M&M's were long gone. Bryn drank the last swallow of water in her poly bottle. It tasted dank and radiated chill.

"A sonata fell in love with a kangaroo," said Sara, beginning a new story. She paused. "I see the shape of trees."

"Like a ponk of ghosts around us," said Connor.

They kept trudging, slower now, waiting. Bryn saw color, dark green fir needles under heavy burdens of snow.

They stopped at Piccadilly Circus. "Snertzola!" said Connor. He pointed with his ski pole. Bryn saw the clear contour of an open slope nearby. A tinge of golden light torched the curving top. The stars were fading. They watched the golden light travel down the hill, until they stood squinting in brilliant sunlight.

Bryn looked around her, disoriented. Vision transformed the labyrinth, and the tangle of story channels was gone. The Shambles looked rougher than it had felt, and the Silk Road had lost its glamor. The smooth loop through the Plain of Marathon was smaller than she imagined, and Interstate 80 skimmed the edge of a drop off they hadn't known was there. She didn't recognize some of the paths. Where was Easter Island? Or Fester City?

Bryn was strangely reluctant to leave. It felt like a loss of something immutable and precious. "*Carpe diem*," she said, "or rather *carpe noctem*. We seized the night."

Sara twirled her poles. "There's tomato soup in the car. Let's go." She led the way. Sara was the best at breaking into new rhythms.

They plowed through untouched snow, skiing easily with the light to their left. Bryn wasn't tired or hungry or thirsty.

Within an hour, she heard the swoosh of a car ahead, and a few minutes later they came out at the top of the steep bank down to Highway 20.

"Pergamobilia!" shouted Connor. He pushed off and glided diagonally down. Bryn followed and then Sara.

They took off their skis and climbed over the snowplow berm, gritty with red volcanic gravel. They headed quickly along the road. Walking was a strange rising and falling, boots hitting rough road rather than gliding smoothly over snow. A few cars and trucks went by, not many this early.

A van screeched to a halt in front of them. The side door slid back. Five people jumped out and charged. Bryn cringed back. Then she recognized what they were. Ski patrol. They wore fancy black tights, wind-stopping fleece, and high-tech hats. "We found you!" one of them crowed.

Someone took away Bryn's skis and poles. Someone else escorted her into the van. They drove off, past the snow park only a few hundred feet away. "Our car is there," said Bryn. She yearned for that tomato soup and Cambozola cheese and crackers. She felt her low-blood-sugar crankiness coming on.

They didn't answer but drove on to a low building. Their parents were waiting in a room with beds like a hospital room. Bryn hugged them, and all five of them laughed a little, half embarrassed.

They were told to lie down. They were covered with blankets, given water and power bars. The water tasted like plastic and the power bar like cardboard, but it staved off the grouchiness.

"We saved the boeuf bourguignon," said Mom.

"We skied out looking for you," said Dad. "All the way to that high meadow off the trail."

"We heard your whistle," Bryn murmured. Her parents had had to survive the night, too.

"Sorry," said Connor. "Sorry to scrumble you, all of you."

But the ski patrol were exultant. "No problem," said a tall girl with no body fat. "We needed the practice. Hardly ever happens."

A newspaper reporter came in. The ski patrol told them all about the three siblings lost overnight in the wilderness. Without a compass. Without a flashlight. Without matches. Without their phones.

The reporter interviewed them with leading questions, trying to pour their mid-winter night into a rigid mold of guilt. "Were you frightened? What would you advise other skiers? How could you have been better prepared? How did you survive?"

The reporter tried to make them say that they should have carried a compass and a flashlight and matches, that they should have had more food and clothes, that they should have turned back earlier.

Bryn spoke for all of them. "We were together. All we needed were peanut M&M's, lebkuchen, and a labyrinth of stories."

Mama Only Visits When It's Dark
(continued)

by Frances Lu-Pai Ippolito

Xiao-yu was asleep by the end of the story when an unbidden breeze began to blow in the bedroom. A-gong looked up as the wind stirred the blanket and ruffled Xiao-yu's hair. On the bed, the rise and fall of the boy's chest was too slight to see under the covers.

I suspected, but now I know for sure, A-gong thought as he glanced at the closed bedroom windows and door where no natural wind could seep through. *There isn't much time to waste. A-yu can't do this much longer.*

The old man groaned at the clicks and aches in his knees when he got up from the bed and hobbled back to the desk. He crumpled and threw away the torn paper and pulled a length of fresh paper from the roll. A pocket knife came out of his pants, and he sliced a sheet that was long enough to cover the desk. With his palms, he smoothed the edges of the cut paper.

"Too small," he muttered when he slid his slender but tall frame into the child's green plastic chair.

On the desk, the ink water in the stone saucer had dried and the brush tip was hard—the hairs stuck together. A-gong opened a bottle of water and dribbled two capfuls into the stone saucer to reawaken and bring the ink back to life. The breeze blew again and picked at the edges of the sheet.

"Humph." A-gong shook his head and put cups of pencils and markers on top of the moving paper to keep the sheet from lifting. Then he pulled up his sleeves and dipped the brush in the watery ink.

In flowing arcs and graceful sweeps, he drew, withdrew, pushed, pulled, and ran the brush from paper's end to paper's end, lifting his brush tip only once. When he finished painting the strokes, he leaned back to look at his work.

Meigui. Rose. His daughter's name.

He set the brush down on the jade stand and waited. The unnatural wind returned and greeted him like a cat, stroking his face and rubbing his white hair. By his ear, he heard it whistle and purr. On the paper, the ink lines unraveled and loosened from their words. They slithered and circled like eels all over the page and then paused in the center to twist into springs.

A-gong continued to wait patiently, allowing the ink to decide what new things to say and share. The lines spiraled, swam, and collided into each other, nudging and jockeying one another aside for space until they found (or maybe remembered) their places.

Baba. Father. I've missed you.

A-gong shut his eyes and tears dropped onto and then into the rice paper.

"I've missed you too," he wrote across a blank space on the bottom of the paper.

This is wonderful. We can be together again.

"Meigui—" he wanted to write, but before the ink touched the paper, Meigui took it straight from the brush tip and pulled them to draw her new words.

Like I never died.

Instead of writing back, A-gong set the brush back on the stand and said aloud, "It's time to let Xiao-yu go. Untether yourself from his life."

Bu. No. The strokes were huge, and the word filled the full sheet of paper, using all the ink.

"He can't sustain you both."

He's strong. He can.

A-gong shook his head. "You know that no living creature can keep itself and a ghost alive, especially a child. A ghost is always hungry."

No.

"Can't you see? You're sucking him dry."

NO! The ink lines sprung out of control, racing off the paper and jumping onto the wall behind the desk. Worms made from shadows twisted and writhed on the cream paint. Unmoored from the page, the shadows climbed to the ceilings and lengthened like claws to stripe the wall next to the sleeping boy.

"Stop!"

NO.

The wind rose once more, knocking the books off the shelves, opening them to opaque pages. The marks from the black crayons, markers, and pencil lead were released from the paper and bled onto the floorboards, drowning it in darkness. A violent whirlpool opened and churned there. A-gong lifted his feet to avoid touching the darkness and shivered as the room temperature dropped below freezing. The darkness grew and midnight tendrils crept up the legs of Xiao-yu's bed, reaching across the blanket for the child's throat.

Along the ceiling molding, Meigui wrote, **I'm scared to be alone.**

A-gong grabbed his brush. What could he say? He was scared, too. Scared for Xiao-yu and scared if he didn't push Meigui to leave, he'd be burying his grandson soon.

"Were you listening to the story?" he wrote.

The inky lines paused on Xiao-yu's shoulders.

You told me the story before.

"Did you understand?"

The lines lay still. Unmoving.

"Did you understand?"

Silence.

"Let him go."

He needs me. I need him.

"He has me and Cliff. We'll love him. You know that."

You lied to him about the end of the story. You changed it.

"I lied to you, too, and told you the truth when you were older."

It was a bad ending. Everyone died.

"Is that what you want?"

At that moment, the boy whispered, "Mama," in his sleep. His breath frosted in the chilled air, and his chest hitched, his inhale uneven and broken.

The lines pushed forward and then away from the boy like ocean waves at a shore.

Promise me, you'll take care of him.

"I promise."

After several long seconds, the lines finally retreated from the bed, down from the walls, back into the book pages and onto the sheet lying across the desk.

Some of the lines paused on the wall behind the desk and rearranged themselves. A face appeared.

A-gong reached out and brushed his fingers against his daughter's face. She smiled and then disappeared when the lines fell off the wall, back onto the rice paper.

"Gong-gong, what's the matter?" Xiao-yu sat up in the bed to find his grandfather weeping at the desk. He hurried up and hugged A-gong. "Don't cry. It'll be ok. I'll do a better job painting, I promise. Can I try again?"

A-gong sniffed and held the boy tight. Already his body felt warm and filled up—solid on the inside again. A-gong guided the boy onto his lap and cut a fresh sheet of paper. He handed the boy the brush.

"Don't squeeze," he said, unclamping the boy's thumb and index finger that strangled the brush's throat. "Don't force the ink. Guide the flow. Be pliant and forgiving. Be flexible. And learn that sometimes you have to let go."

Halftime
(continued)

by Susan Hammerman

Detective Barns didn't break eye contact with Lynne as he spoke.

When he finished, Lynne said, "My sister didn't do anything wrong."

"You aren't betraying Elaine. You're just going to tell me what happened," Detective Barns said, like it would be easy for her. "Okay. Time for the truth, Lynne. Your sister discovered Jolie's dead body in the parking lot. Not you, right? And Elaine had to ask you to call the police for her. She couldn't because she is having an affair with Jolie's husband, Peter."

Lynne needed him to stop hounding her and shut up.

"Come on!" He banged his fist on the table. "Let go, Lynne. Admit it. Elaine found Jolie's body, right?"

Lynne nodded, leaned forward, and rested her head on the table. She was exhausted.

"It's okay. I understand," he said.

Lynne was certain that he didn't. She told him what he wanted to hear.

Lynne stepped out of the taxi and glanced up at the balcony of her apartment. The petunias looked droopy in their bright ceramic pots. They needed water. Thinking back, she couldn't remember which had come first, discovering that Miss Goody Two-Shoes was having an affair with a married man or noticing, when she was potting the flowers, that the building's security camera was within easy reach of her balcony. Everything had fallen into place after that.

Lynne opened her mailbox and got her mail, one business envelope. Maybe it was halftime that set the plan in motion. Elaine mentioned it when

Lynne borrowed a jacket from her for an interview that didn't go well. Lynne hadn't thought about halftime in years. That detail put flesh on her character's bones.

Her acting teacher told her to live the role — think, walk, eat, speak, dream in character. The instructor said to build the character from true feelings and real memories, brick by brick, like a house, a house the actor inhabits from the roof all the way down to the foundation. Lynne thought the character she created would always be a part of her, but without noticing when it happened, Lynne left her behind.

The method acting classes were expensive, but ended up being a great investment, and cheaper than the iPad, which Lynne couldn't keep. She couldn't keep the security camera either. It was the same model as the building's and was now smashed to pieces, along with the iPad, and dumped across town.

Through trial and error, using her security camera, she managed to make the video running on the iPad look passable as live footage on the building's security camera. She'd fooled around with dangling the iPad on wire and a coat hanger, but a selfie stick tied to a post on her balcony worked perfectly. The potted flowers camouflaged it from the street.

Lynne pushed the elevator button for her floor. No, it was the gun that had clinched it. Taking Dad's gun, well, Dad would call it stealing. Stealing his gun was the final detail that made the plan work. The gun was not hidden across town. It was dropped within easy walking distance of Elaine's place. The police had it now. Lynne unlocked her apartment door. Convincing Jolie to meet had been the hardest part. Jolie didn't believe Peter was cheating on her. The first shot was hard. The second was easier.

That day, after Lynne got back to her place, and after she called the police, she called her mother. She called her knowing it would be the last time her mother would ask her why she couldn't be more like her sister. After Elaine's arrest, the threats to cut her off and cut her out of the will ended. Lynne tore open the envelope and pulled out a trust fund check.

Voices Carry
(continued)

by Barb Lachenbruch

Family! I sighed. No matter where I directed my stories, they always came back to family, whether I wanted them to or not.

But the story had done its job. It had taken long enough. I'd made it all the way to our exit, and then to town streets. Three miles to go. And Gary never did offer to help.

Incredible how men could be.

I pulled into our driveway.

"I could tell we were almost here," Benjamin said, "from the stoplights."

"I could too," Elspeth said.

I whispered, "Let's be quiet. Your dad's still sleeping. You can go in and sleep, or eat breakfast, or watch a video. I want to lie down." I was so sleepy.

I preceded them to the house to unlock the door, then returned to the car. Gary hadn't moved. "You can keep sleeping," I told him. "The kids are in. I'm going upstairs." I closed the car door quietly, then dragged myself inside and up the stairs to the bed.

I slept, but not much. In an hour, the kids were in the bedroom asking if we had any bread. I sat up crossly. I couldn't remember what was in the house. We'd left eight days before. "Can't you ask your dad?"

"He's not there," Benjamin said.

He must have gone to the office. Of all things. He should have taken the kids to the pool, or somewhere—to let me sleep after my all-nighter.

"The VHS isn't working again," Elspeth said.

My head was in the basement freezer when the phone rang. I ran up the stairs to catch it.

"Well?" said a voice. "Are you coming back or not?" It was Gary.

"Where are you?"

"Where am I? Where do you think? I stepped out to pee. Lucky, I'd grabbed your fleece. You just zoomed away."

Almost eight hours before.

I was already blaming him for his asinine quietness. This never would have happened if Gary had talked.

But he'd screw this around to blaming me.

Then I pictured him at the side of the road in my little pink fleece with the appliquéd bears. He'd always hated that jacket on me. I stifled a laugh. "I'll—I'll call the highway patrol and ask them to drive you home," I said.

He hung up.

Like that's fair. What was I supposed to do now?

I called the sheriff. They said I had to call California, not Oregon. California said, "We got no one anywhere near."

I paced. Went to the car. It was true: my jacket was missing. But his wallet and shoes were still here. My spirits sank. And that fleece: it was hopeless in the rain.

I carried loads in from the car, then from the RocketBox. I unpacked luggage. Started laundry.

Still the phone didn't ring.

I made coffee. Cleaned the VHS player, dirty from the library videos. I moved the laundry to the dryer, started a second load. Watered the houseplants, put the first load away. Moved the second load. Started the third. Threw out junk mail.

The phone rang again. The kids gathered to watch. "I'm at the gas station two exits south of ours. This drunk guy gave me a freezing ride in the back of his pick-up. Next to an open gas can, I almost puked the whole way. He asked if I could chip in for gas, but before I called you last time, there was less than a buck in your pocket."

And a tampon, I realized.

"I gave him thirteen cents." He called off to someone, "I'll be there," then said, "He ended up giving me the money to call you. Says he'll leave me at our exit in a half hour."

"Let's meet at the diner," I was saying as he hung up. "Kids, let's go."

The three of us arrived first. Would he laugh when he came in? I tried to make a light mood, but the kids would not go along. They must have been tired from the night.

We'd half-eaten our meals when Gary arrived. He stood, theatrically, at the diner's door—and he was not laughing. Benjamin strode to him with his shoes and dry socks. I nodded to the waitress to bring his meal, but we had a misunderstanding; she had not yet placed the order, so when Gary appeared, we had to wait.

No one talked much.

Finally, Gary said, "I walked to the rest area, then stood by the drinking fountains. I thought you'd be back."

"Was it raining?" I asked.

He glared.

"I thought you were in the sleeping bag," I said. This would be my chance, my one chance, to bend his interpretation to mine. "I told you I was going to pee. You didn't tell me you were going to pee. You were already almost asleep. I thought you dove over and were in the back. That's what a person would do."

"I asked for rides," he told me. "One guy said, 'Your story sounds too weird.' Like he thought I was abusing you, and you threw me out."

I looked at the kids, who should not have been hearing this. Gary did not.

We made it through breakfast. I paid. I let him drive, one hand, thumb inside the wheel.

And to top it off, Gary got the first shower. I called around, found an open store, drove there, bought wine and veggies for the party, and frozen pizza for the kids.

After my shower, I made little appetizers while Gary went on the computer and caught up with work. I could hear the kids' video from the kitchen. I put the second and third loads of laundry away as the pizza baked. I was exhausted. The evening passed more slowly than his drive and mine combined. When it was finally 9:00, the sitter arrived.

On the way to the party I said, "It'll be funny to tell everyone what happened, don't you think?"

"Don't you breathe a word of it," Gary spit.

He'd have his version. His version would be wrong.

I held my version in, until finally, on a family trip to New York, I confessed it all to my old college roommate so she could tell me I was right. "At the incredible very least," I said, "he should have told me he was getting out to pee."

"Don't worry. Truth finds its way out," she said. "He's the criminal. Yours is the perfect crime."

That afternoon in the elevator back up to her apartment, I overheard two people talking. "You'll never believe what I heard this morning. This lady left her husband at a rest area. For seven hours without knowing it. But it was actually his fault."

Yes. Voices carry.

A Visitor on a Rainy Night
(continued)

by Karen Eisenbrey

Chamokat waited without speaking to be sure Stell had finished her story. The fire broke the silence with a loud pop. They both jumped and shared a smile of embarrassment.

"Thank you for this tale," Chamokat said. "It explains much. Your people are strange; stranger than I thought before." He rose reluctantly. "I will leave you now."

"It is late and still raining," Stell protested. "Stay the night at least. You may have Crane's room."

"I am honored," he replied.

Chamokat rose before dawn the next morning. Crane's bed was not what he was used to, but comfortable, and sleeping under a roof was better than camping in the rain. His people were taught from infancy to distrust the Eukardians, to keep hidden from them and have nothing to do with them. Especially with their wizards. But if this one woman could welcome an Aklaka stranger so warmly, how bad could they be?

Stell was already in the kitchen when he came out of his room. She greeted him with the smile of an old friend. "I thought you might be off early. Did you sleep well?"

"Yes, thank you. But it seems best to go before people are out." He didn't want to force himself or his new ideas on anyone before they were ready. Especially anyone who would see him as a monster.

"You remind me of someone else who never wants to be seen," she said. "I'll send some food with you."

He gladly accepted the bread and dried fruit, passing over the cheese. He still had dried meat and smoked fish of his own. He would be able to feed himself until he rejoined his band in a day or two. He offered Stell a portion of the fish. "I should have given you this last night. Aklaka never arrive empty-handed."

"If you can spare it, I gladly accept." She sniffed it and smiled. "I don't plan to share it. It's not often I get a treat to enjoy by myself."

"Thank you for your hospitality, Mamam Stell." Chamokat donned his cedar-bark hat. The rain had stopped, but it would keep off the sun as well. He rolled up the cape and stowed it in his bag. "I did not know what to expect. I am glad I took the chance."

"As am I, Chamokat," Stell said. "Any friend of Crane's is welcome here. I hope you will return someday."

Chamokat left the big stone dwelling with the heron painted on its sign. He had previously seen Eukardian houses only from a distance. Such strange dwellings, built of trees and stones. They both permanent and vulnerable, solid but standing out in the open for all to see. Not like the hidden dugout lodges and subtly painted tents of the Aklaka. Now he could say he had slept inside one and come to no harm.

It was thrilling to walk in the open so near a Eukardian settlement. Aklaka learned early how to avoid notice, but it was easier in the deep or dappled shade of a forest than in this grassland. He passed through an open pasture near Stell's house and followed the river toward the sparse growth of timber to the west. He should reach there before the sun was high, and then he would be out of sight.

This visit had been a good idea for more reasons than he had intended. He had meant only to meet his friend's mother, give her what news he could, and satisfy his own curiosity about these people who lived beside him but separately. Now an unforeseen plan took shape. Chamokat could not execute this plan on his own. He would play the role of advocate for a radical idea.

Chamokat's father, the leader of their band, had his "small friend" of mixed Aklaka and Eukardian heritage, and in Crane, Chamokat did, too. That kind of mixing, the kind that produced children, had always gone on around the fringes. Why not also open friendship? Why not trade in goods, knowledge … and stories?

He would share with his father what he had learned. Especially the story, or as much of it as he could remember and translate. There was more to these Eukardians than he had ever dreamed. To be fair, most of them did not know the Aklaka existed, which meant there was more to his own people, too. *Someone who never wants to be seen.* Chamokat no longer wanted that. Was it not better to be seen, to speak with their own voice, than be a myth, a tale, a rumor? There were plenty of stories. They did not need to be one more.

Dadad would want to know, and his sister Kala. She would inherit leadership someday. And she was as fond of Crane as Chamokat was. Fonder, in fact. But the vision did not show him returning to her. Too bad Crane would not be Chamokat's actual brother.

The idea couldn't be rushed. A few Aklaka would be more ready than most; others would prefer to do things as they always had. Crane's presence among them had made that divide plain, though he looked almost like one of them and had done no harm to anyone; and he was one of the hated wizards. He had volunteered for a dangerous task. If he accomplished it, no one would have to risk it ever again. With that argument in favor, most of Chamokat's people would surely come around.

Sooner or later, it would be time for the Aklaka to emerge from the shadows. Why not start now? Better to do it on their own terms. To stop hiding and meet the Eukardians in the open. As equals.

Kanareyka

(continued)

by Rick M. Cook

Freddy's breathing grew ragged in the eerie stillness
of the mining tunnel. How he had the strength to tell
such detailed and engrossing stories, one inside the
other, I'll never understand. Maybe it was his D&D
training, his love for spinning tales, but the light within
his eyes had grown with intensity as he weaved
through the labyrinth of stories, almost as if he
possessed some of Crane's wizardry or had eaten all
of those life-sustaining *lebkuchen*.

But now he complained of tingling in his hands and feet. How could he feel anything below his waist when everything there was crushed flat under the boulder?

Bittersweetness swelled in my heart. "Freddy, why did you choose those stories?"

Silent, he gathered his strength to respond. Telling those tales had taken a lot out of him. "Doesn't matter, Mandy. Not anymore."

Determined to encourage him to hold on, I said, "I'm not a brainiac like you, but I think I know why. You're like those mountain people, the Aklaka. Shy, quiet, mysterious. Wanting to be understood but afraid to be at the same time. I understand that now."

He wriggled and tried to interrupt me, but I stroked his hair to calm him, his head still sitting in my lap, and continued.

"Yes, we are lost like those kids in a mountain blizzard. But they found their way home, and so will we. Don't give up, Freddy! We'll get you to a hospital. And I swear to Christ, I will *not* leave your side to get dinner and miss the moment you come back to us."

I was almost ranting, trying to convince myself more than Freddy.

As death approached, his body continued to shut down. Maybe that's why he seemed to feel less pain now. I wanted to scream again about how wrong all of this was.

Guilt consumed me. Was Freddy saying we'd been like that couple driving back from California who sucked at communication? Probably so. But that was in my past. I could change, be a better person.

God, please let him live! I promise I'll be the best friend to him. Let me trade my soul in a Devil's deal—steal a valuable bottle of wine if that's what it takes—just save him.

Shock settled on me as the point of his other story pricked my brain. Was he telling me it was okay to move on from this life, like A-gong did to his daughter, Meigui? No, I could not accept that. I would not accept that. My mind reeled, but I knew we'd make it out of the cave together.

I wiped at the sweat gathering on his forehead and tried to keep him warm, his mind off the pain. He shivered again. I wished we had that pink fleece jacket, even if it had appliquéd bears on it.

He stirred. "The stories are just something for you … to remember me by … I know I'm dying."

"You're not going to die, Freddy. We'll get out of this and make it safely back to our parents, just like Bryce and his sister did in your story."

He glared at me. "Cut the bullcrap, Mandy. We both know that's not true." His eyes pierced my soul. "Here, now—*especially now*—can't we just be honest with each other?"

I was taken aback by his sudden directness and angry voice. They say the spirit puts up one last fight before giving up entirely. Maybe this was his last stand. I prayed I'd have the strength to match his, to be there for him when he needed me most. But the knots in my stomach put that into serious doubt.

"You're right," I said. "Let's be honest." I smiled faintly. "You go first."

He smirked. "Fine, fraidy-cat."

"Just don't say nerdy things like '*Carpe Diem*,' okay?"

"I wasn't."

"I hate French."

"It's Latin," he said and closed his eyes. In the dim light of my iPhone, a ghostly white had settled on his face. Life was fading from him.

That's when his breathing stopped. My fingers dashed to his neck and pressed for a pulse. It was still there but faint.

"You know," he said, coming to and looking at my bloodied fingers and broken nails. "With claws like that, you'll never make Homecoming Queen."

I could have punched him for scaring me. Instead, I pouted for effect. "Honestly?"

"Honestly."

"Dude, you're such a catty bitch."

He tried to laugh, but it came out as a wheeze. His throat had gone dry, making it difficult for him to swallow. I took the scrunchie from my ponytail, poured water over it, and made a sort of sponge for him to suck on. Anything to keep from dwelling on the thought that I might die here with him.

"You'll get out alive," he said, seeming to read my mind. "Since we're being honest, I have to tell you something else."

I shook my head. "Freddy, you don't have to—"

"No, I gotta." He coughed and spat up some blood. "We only have today, right now. I'm at negative five and draining fast."

I cocked my head inquisitively and squinted at him while cleaning his face.

"It's a D&D term," he explained. "Look, there's things I wanted to say to you for a long time … but I was afraid. I'm not afraid anymore."

Petrified at what he might tell me, I turned away to wipe at the tears burning my eyes, but he grabbed my hand.

"Mandy, you are *my* Valentina, my unvoiced love. You're the funniest and prettiest girl at school. Bad as you might pretend to be, you're a good person deep down. I know you know I think you're beautiful, both inside and out, but you need to hear it. You need to *know* it."

His strength was fading, but somehow, sheer will power seemed to drive him on.

"Being around you makes me … happy. Even now, as The Unkissable Geek who's loved you for so long … even dying here … there's no one else I'd rather be with."

He still gripped my hand, but I managed to push back tears with the other.

"Freddy," I mumbled, squeezing his hand. "I don't know what else to say but thank you."

His shoulders sagged, and he gave a wistful smile, disappointed in my answer. Clearly, he hoped for more.

"Hey," I began. "We said no bullshit, right?"

"Right," he answered. "Real friends tell each other the truth."

"Yeah." I breathed in deeply and sighed. "I've been a jerk to you."

I moved a lock of blond hair out of his eyes and continued. "You've always been able to see me. When Nana was in the hospital, you were there for me. Same for the time my brother was in that car accident. When the 'cool kids' ragged on me, you *always* stuck up for me. And you helped me so many times with my stupid English and geometry homework, though I still don't know what a fucking arctangent is."

"It's the inverse—"

"Shh," I said, pressing an index finger to his lips. "That doesn't matter right now. What *does* matter is that I see you for the incredible person you are. You've never asked for anything in return. I've been an asshole, and I'm sorry. I wish I could go back and be kinder to you. I'm sorry for not sticking up for you when other kids made fun of you. I wish …"

"Yeah?" Freddy said, just above a whisper, his pupils as big as saucers and his breathing shallower.

"I wish we had more time. I'd like to know you better."

Freddy's breathing paused again and fell silent. A fright ran through me. He was slipping away. Half a minute passed with no movement of his chest. Then, it rose again.

"Mandy, I can't see. You still here?"

"I'm here. Can't you feel my hands?" I squeezed him and stroked his face. His eyelids fluttered shut.

"Yes." He paused. When he opened them again, his eyes stared past me, unfocused. "I'd love to see your face once more, but I can't." His breathing slowed. "Also, I lied … I *am* afraid … scared as hell."

"Me too," I said. "But I'm here."

"Thank you." His chest fell flat, then fluttered again. "I lied … twice … Earlier, I did want to say *Carpe Diem*."

"Oh, Freddy," I cried, bending over and hugging him.

I kissed him right then, not wanting the moment to slip past. My tears ran down onto his face and mixed with his. He kissed me back with all his fading strength, his last breath passing between those beautiful lips and into the stillness of the cave.

Strange how, at the moment of his death, I had never felt so alive. And I've never been kissed like that since.

The Tale of the Tape
(continued)

by Mark Teppo

Flap. Flap. Flap.

The tape has run out. The reel keeps spinning, the end of the tape flapping against the machinery. She sits, silent. Her face is wet with tears. Her hands are in her lap.

In the hall, the grandfather clock is unmoved by what it has heard. *Tock. Tock. Tock.*

She shifts. Sighs. Her throat works, but nothing comes out of her mouth. Not yet. She isn't ready.

She stops the machine. Her hand shakes a little as she pulls the reel off the spindle. She puts the reel into its box, and she slips the box into the pocket of her jacket. Her hand lingers for a moment, feeling the weight of what she carries, of the circular recursion hidden within the story.

It is too long, filled with lumbering asides and complicated anecdotes. The sort of tale that, were it to be told in the back room at the Magpie's Charm, would be met with cries of derision. *Get to the point!* the crowd would holler. Every storyteller—even the untrained, untested, and unlettered ones— knows that control of your audience hangs on your ability to keep the story moving. But this story is not meant for the telling. It is a secret, and like all secrets, its truth is obscured and complicated.

But she knows the origin of this tale, and that is enough to unlock the secret of what is kept on this tape. And the secret, having been heard—not once, but twice, and isn't that enough in the telling?—is a secret no longer. It is hers once again.

She leaves the safe open. It is a slip, an error that would make Remejin cluck his tongue at her negligence. *We are invisible*, he would say. *If they don't know we were there, they can't tell stories about us.*

She doesn't care. "Let them talk," she says later when she meets Remejin in the hidden room at the Charm.

He smiles at the sound of her voice.

Storytellers

(continued)

by Benjamin Gorman

Can I get another? This one's just melted ice now.
Thanks.

Thanks.

Don't worry, Danique. I'll drink this one faster.
And then we'll go back to your cabin. I wasn't going
to tell you this whole thing and then just leave. That
would feel wrong, you know? I knew before I started
telling the story how the story of this night was
supposed to end. As soon as you asked to buy me a
drink and tell you my best story. You asked for a

story, so I knew you were for me. Of course I knew the story of tonight. And you did, too. That's the point. We know how we want the story to work. And maybe you'll look back on it and say, "I met the weirdest woman in a bar on Eridani d. She made me listen to this long, rambling story before she came back to my cabin."

Well, of course you say that now.

Maybe you're just being nice. But you'll also say, "She was amazing in bed, so it was worth it."

But maybe later you'll think about the whole story. Tonight, sure. You'll remember tonight, I promise. But my grandpa's story inside this story. And all the stories inside his story. And it will click. I'm not saying you don't understand it now. But I hope you'll understand it more deeply later. When something happens that doesn't make sense. You'll be sad and angry, pissed off at the universe, and I want you to be able to pull back from that and say, "Why am I pissed? Why am I not just accepting that this is the way things are, chaotic and meaningless and cold?" Because you could. That might be true. But it would be true of the universe, not true of you, of me, of all us humans. We want the story. We burn for it. We bite our own tails and hold on and chew like animals with a paw caught in a trap. And that's miserable and it's gross, I know. But when things are bad, maybe we can celebrate the strength of our desire for the story to be better.

Because that's why we're here. That's why we're on Eridani d. That's why you'll be in my arms tonight. That's what my grandpa wanted me to understand. It's not whether the stories are true. It's that we want the story to be right.

Okay, pay the lady, and let's get outta here.

About the Authors

Gabby Gilliam lives in the DC metro area. Her poetry has most recently appeared in *Tofu Ink Arts Press*, *Tempered Runes Press*, *Cauldron Anthology*, *Instant Noodles*, and two anthologies from *Mythos Poets Society*. Her short fiction appeared in the *Bones* anthology from Black Hare Press.

Debby Dodds is the author of the novel *Amish Guys Don't Call* named a BEST YA OF 2017 by Powell's Books and it was featured in Random House's *Better with Books: Diverse Books to Ignite Empathy*. She was awarded a 2021 Fellowship to MVICW. She's had over 25 short stories and essays published in anthologies including the NY Times best-selling *My Little Red Book* (Twelve/

Hachette) and in The Sun Magazine. She has her BFA from NYU and MFA from Antioch University. She teaches Creative Writing through many programs including Oregon State University's TAG program, Sunshine Elite Academy, and Catlin Gabel School. As an actress, she wrote and performed in stage shows at both Disneyland and Disney World and she screamed in B-horror films.

Ann Ornie is an Oregonian, lover of old trees, the desert, and is a National Park enthusiast. When she isn't writing or reading she can be found rambling through the woods on an adventure with her husband, son, and dog named Lucy.

You can find her work in *The North Coast Squid Literary Magazine*, *Rain Magazine*, *NIWA's 2020 Anthology*, "Escape," and the recently published anthology, *The Phone*. She is the 2019 Haunted Astoria Writer's Showcase Winner and the Writer and Producer of the Cold Coast Podcast. You can visit her website at: www.annornie.com and follow her on Instagram: @treesifyouplease.

Dr. Bunny McFadden is a Chicana mother and educator of pirates and sea monsters (and children) in San Francisco. You can spot more of her work in JSTOR, various horror and sci-fi anthologies, and a few other places.

LM Zaerr is a writer of fiction for teens and adults. She taught medieval literature and music at Boise State University. As a professor, she lured students into medieval tales and abandoned them there to challenge dragons, rescue Lancelot, and figure out how to play Gwyddbwyll. She wrote a book on medieval storytelling, and she memorized forgotten tales in dusty languages and sang them to the raucous tones of the vielle. Now she finds new stories dripping with sunshine and sword polish.

Frances Lu-Pai Ippolito is a Chinese American writer based in Portland, Oregon. When she's not spending time with her family outdoors, she's crafting short stories in horror, sci-fi, fantasy, or whatever genre-bending she can get away with. Her writing has appeared in Nailed Magazine, Red Penguin's Collections, and Buckman Journal's Issue 006. Her work will also be included in Flame Tree Press's *Asian Ghost Stories* and Strangehouse's *Chromophobia*. She can be found at www.francesippolito.com.

Susan Hammerman, a former rare book librarian, writes crime and neo-noir short stories. Her stories have been published by Mystery Magazine, Dark City Mystery Magazine, Blood and Bourbon, Mondays are Murder, and Retreats From Oblivion. Susan also serves on the national board of Sisters in Crime.

Barb Lachenbruch writes fiction and creative non-fiction that reflects her perpetual astonishment by nature and human nature. She was formerly a professor of wood science and forest biology but now considers herself a botany nerd. She, her husband, and small dog, split time between Corvallis, Oregon, and their off-grid cabin in the Coast Range, where she beats back invasive weeds and dabbles in making maple syrup. She has published in High Country News.

Karen Eisenbrey lives in Seattle, WA, where she leads a quiet, orderly life and invents stories to make up for it. Karen writes fantasy and science fiction novels, as well as short fiction in a variety of genres and the occasional poem or song if it insists. She is the author of five novels: *The Gospel According to St. Rage*; *Barbara and the Rage Brigade*; *Daughter of Magic*; *Wizard Girl*; and *Death's Midwife*, all from Not A Pipe Publishing. Karen shares her life with her husband, two young adult sons, and four feline ghosts.

Rick M. Cook: When he's not writing his debut novel, *The Devil's Bridge*, he is working on one real-life science fiction project after another. He writes and teaches software to help top aerospace and automotive designers around the world wire their vehicles: futuristic all-electric airplanes to airplane seats and control modules to Blackhawk and Chinook helicopters to wiring for the advancement of human knowledge with satellites and space telescopes. Rick has been writing software since he was fifteen and telling stories even longer to entertain himself and friends. A Dungeons & Dragons game exposed his teenage mind to the world of imaginative storytelling, sparking his creativity every day since. He enjoys reading books of history, science fiction/fact, fantasy, thrillers, and has enough Wikipedia tabs open to support a small invading alien army's intel. He lives in Beaverton, Oregon, along with his wife and two bundles of fun masquerading as dogs. Find him at https://linktr.ee/RickMCook.

Mark Teppo divides his time between Portland and Sumner, and he tends to navigate by local bookstore positioning. He writes historical fiction, fantasy, speculative fiction, and horror, and has published more than a dozen novels. If he's writing a mystery, he's pretending to be Harry Bryant. He also runs Underland Press, an independent publishing house. You can learn more about him at www.markteppo.com, or follow him on Twitter (@markteppo) or Instagram (@mark.teppo).

Benjamin Gorman is an award-winning high school English teacher, political activist, author, poet, and co-publisher at Not a Pipe Publishing. He lives in Independence, Oregon, with bibliophile and guillotine aficionado Chrystal, his favorite son, Noah, and his dog, E.V. (External Validation). His novels are *The Sum of Our Gods*, *Corporate High School*, *The Digital Storm*, and *Don't Read This Book*. He's also the author of two books of poetry: *When She Leaves Me* and *This Uneven Universe*. He believes in his students and the future they'll create if given the chance.

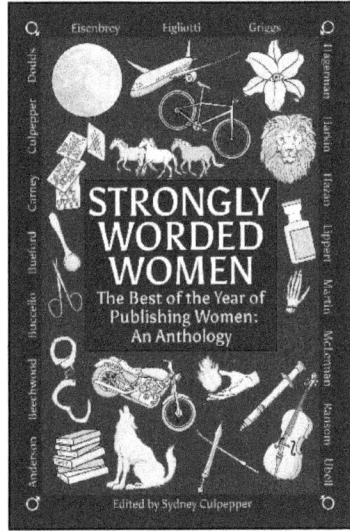

CPSIA information can be obtained
at www.ICGtesting.com
Printed in the USA
BVHW061129190722
642130BV00006BA/118